The Three Vests
The New Brilliants

Special thanks to the original audio production cast
and crew. Without your inspiration, this book would
have never been completed.

Allen and Teresa Larsen at Cascade Recording
Meagan Jones
Matt McMonagle
Kellen Raether
Justin Dennis
Jesse Celaya
Victoria Jones
Andy Arvisu
Natalya Busso

Beta Readers: A special thank you goes to all those kids that read the early versions of this book, offered comments, and ultimately made this book better. Listed are their names.

MEAGAN JONES   JUSTIN DENNIS
ADAM BRANDT   JESSICA REMLEY
TREVER LARKIN   JON GOYT
JESSE CELAYA   CARLOS LIMON
ARTURO HUERTA   MARICELA SALDANA
NOLAN MCMONAGLE   JAIME SILVA
ARMANDO DAVILA   NATALYA BUSSO
REYNA ESCALERA   ALEX DAVILA
JENNY ARELLANO   MELANI GUERRERO
RITCHI REYNOSO   MARIA RENTERIA

Steve Smith   Adam Grandes   Steven Starr
Mike Person   Stephanie Simon   Michelle Dix
Yessica Charero   Kang Chung   Nate Stamen
Trisha Garrison   Michael Jones   Louise Sting
Amy Lunt   Cecil Bridges   Tom Bates
Phillip Coffman   Gilden Givens   Dan Cole
John Colpitts   Eric Luebke   Dan Battis
Susan Susisk   Carl Douglas   Penny Beck
Alisa Cashman   Sue Carver   Craig Betts

What people have said about
The Three Vests — The New Brilliants

"This book is really good! I love to read, but the book has to grab me from the start and hold on all the way through . . . your book did this. I'm looking forward to reading more of your work."

-Terry Larkin

"It's mystery, action, adventure, and humor all mixed into one suspenseful novel that keeps you coming back for more!"

- The Jon G. Book Review

"I loved this book because it sounded like it was written from a teen point of view and the way they look at life."

- Melani Guerrero

"The book has humor, action, fantasy, adventure . . . and mixes it all up to make an awesome adventure."

- Jesse Celaya

"The difference between this book and others is it's not too childish, with the fights . . . also the good guys don't win in two seconds."

- Adam Brandt

"I liked this book because it had comedy and action. My favorite part of the book was when Juan was invisible in the locker room with Josh Zimmerman . . ."

- Nolan McMonagle

"I liked how this book is something totally new! I also liked how it made you ask questions and how it was mysterious."

- Natalya Busso

"I really liked this book because it had two of my most favorite things . . . action and comedy."

- Carlos Limon

"The thing that makes this book good is that it hooks you from beginning to end."

- Trever Larkin

More Beta Readers:

Micheal Kitts	Fred Gorhum	Lisa Davy
Paul Cassel	Elizabeth Cendejas	Vane Britt
Brittney Caris	Theo Brock	Lynn Bears
John Garmley	Maxwell Morrison	Cary Pygot
Kingren Terry	Silvia Martinez	Billy Taylor
Douglas Symonds	Faith Maxwell	Greg Taylor
Parris Stotts	Sergio Rybakov	Lisa Riggs
Pat Grentz	Shane Urwin	Craig Wallace
Cassandra Willet	Freddy Wilder	Ray Price
John Zook	Tommy Vegdahl	Gary Zook
Magdalena Valdez	Harris Brinks	Laura Kale
Laura Montoya	Madonna Moore	Tom Moon
Parker McFarland	Peter McFarland	Don Jems
Sly McDonald	John White	Steve White
Herbert Wallace	Lorna Whitney	Greg Carry
David Darrington	John Barry	Jason Sweeny
Mike Johnson	Kay Nigis	Terry Zane
Tammi Smith	Charles Smith	Walden Sern
Aaron Strauser	Tatiyana Salsibury	Alicia Robb
Kathy Robertson	Roman Dedicino	Albert Rank
Jessie Moran	Joaquin Sanchez	Tracy Lloyd
Eric Mattews	Frances Luken	Rick Ingram
Don Griffin	Cindy Green	Royce Gladis

For the students who believed and listened.

To my wife — who encouraged.

Edited by: Merry Roy - Sharon Young - Marilyn Weishaar

ISBN 0-9713530-2-6
Library of Congress Control Number: 2002096095

Printed in the United States

This is a first edition. Fall 2003.

The Three Vests
The New Brilliants

Robert Bowman

Smart and Smarter Publishing

Orondo, Washington

The Adenture is About to Begin

Chapter One
Boulder Cave

Samantha Banks, George Luisi, and Juan Ramirez stood at the entrance of Boulder Cave, aptly named because the opening looked as though someone had chiseled it out of a giant boulder. Dozens of snowberry bushes and tall tamarack trees bordered the sides of the entryway, and if you didn't know where to look, it would be easy to miss.

Boulder Cave was an obscure grotto. In the dozens of times Samantha, George, and Juan had been there, not once had they seen another person. And it was on a late Sunday afternoon in the last weekend of September that the three friends found themselves staring into its darkness as cold air brushed into their faces like icy needles.

If this expedition was anything like the one they had taken last weekend, they would stay until nearly dark before heading back to the trail where George's father would pick them up at a turnout on State Route 97 promptly at eight.

None of them had any indication that this day was going to be different — that something miraculous and mysterious was about to take place. The weather was similar to what it had been all week. It was warm; temperatures were in the mid-eighties, quite normal for central Washington state. The skies were clear, and a soft wind blew along the top of the canyon wall where they had taken the trail that descended into the cave.

Each of them carried the necessary equipment for amateur spelunking . . . a warm coat and a powerful waterproof flashlight stocked with freshly charged D batteries, along with a water bottle that holstered at the belt. Each wore a wristwatch that glowed with an indigo light, giving them the ability to see the time even in complete darkness.

"Five o'clock," Juan said, looking at his watch quickly. "Got up here too late. We won't be able to get to Cavern C and get back in time to meet your dad, George."

George looked at Juan and nodded his head in agreement. Juan, along with Samantha, were George's closest friends. He had grown up with them since preschool and knew their parents so well it was as though they were all family. In fact, George and Juan were often mistaken for brothers, not because they looked alike, but because they acted alike — their senses of humor and their desires for adventure were just a couple of their shared traits.

Even though both were twelve years old, their physical features were very different. Juan was a round, slightly over-weight preteen with olive skin and dark brown hair that matched his eyes. His nose resembled that of a pug dog; smashed in a bit like someone had hit it with a baseball bat. His hair was cut high and tight along the sides and spiked at the top. He liked this cut the best because it was the only one that went with his round face and puffy cheeks.

George, on the other hand, was bony. His thin, sandy brown hair was long and, as it was most of the time, pulled back in a ponytail. This drove his mother nuts, but he had worn his hair like that ever since fifth grade and wasn't about to change. His bright, sparkling blue eyes were narrow and thoughtful. His sharp nose slanted down to pursed lips and a pimply chin. Like many kids his age, he was struggling with adolescent acne. He didn't like the red blotches that littered his jaw line and cheeks, but there was nothing he could do about it. All the Noxzema in the world wouldn't take the acne away, and he was patient enough to wait until he grew out of them, as his father reminded him from time to time when George complained about his looks.

"So what cavern then?" Samantha asked anxiously, geared up with her flashlight in-hand and ready.

It was George's father who had sparked their interest in exploring. Ever since the kids had been in third grade, he'd taken them to various caves throughout Washington. He avoided the more popular ones, like the Wind River Ice Caves and the Ape Cave near Mount Saint Helens, and instead concentrated on the more remote, hard to reach grottos.

This was the second year that Samantha, George, and Juan were allowed to go into Boulder Cave without George's father, but only when the three were together. They promised their parents that they would never split up once they were inside, and for the most part, kept their pledge.

During the last couple of years they had mapped the enormous cave into three sections: Cavern L, because it took the shape of an L; Cavern U, because it started high, dipped down and back up again, like the letter U; and lastly, Cavern C because it traced the shape of the letter C.

"Yeah, C won't work," George said, thoughtfully. "Let's go with L. We can be outta there by seven, and that'll give us an hour to get back to the road to meet Dad."

"Hope the bats are still there," Juan said, clicking his flashlight on and following Samantha.

"Yeah, that was cool," Samantha whispered as she was the first to be engulfed by complete darkness.

Juan and George trailed her, shining their flashlights in different directions in the cave. Water trickled everywhere, puddling at their feet. They had learned early on that waterproof boots were the only thing to wear if they wanted their feet warm and dry.

The tube — George's name for the initial part of the grotto — was long and narrow. It was only about seven-feet high, and the further it descended, the more cramped it became until by its end they had to duck and shuffle sideways through a small opening. This crack in the rock was an opening to another chamber within the cave and led to Cavern L.

"Did you guys hear Paul yesterday?" Samantha asked irritably, carefully leading the two boys over the jagged rocks and large stones that cluttered the path.

"You mean Friday —" George corrected her. "Yesterday was Saturday."

"Yeah, Friday."

"No, why, what'd he do?" Juan wondered, pointing his flashlight at the ground and trying not to roll an ankle.

"You didn't hear about it?" Samantha asked agitatedly, turning and looking at her friends in stunned surprise. George and Juan stopped as the three of them pointed their flashlights at each other.

"Paul . . . who?" George questioned, having no idea who Samantha was referring to.

"Paul Hertzinger. You know — he's kind of tall, doesn't have a lot of teeth," Juan said, laughingly.

"Oh, yeah," sighed George. "I know who you're talking about. The guy's weird."

"Exactly," Samantha jumped in. "You didn't hear about what he said to Laura Powell?"

"Who?" Again, George was lost.

"George, do you know anybody at school?" Juan joked, shaking his head.

"I have no idea who you're talking about."

"Laura Powell," Samantha said, drawing the last name out emphatically. "Brown hair, toothy girl."

Juan laughed. "Toothy? You describe people as toothy?"

"Well, she is," Samantha answered flatly.

That was just one of the things that Juan and George admired about Samantha. She was honest, and to go along with the honesty, she was a brain. She was by far the smartest of all of them, as her grades in school proved — grades on which she prided herself. Her grade point had never wavered from the perfect 4.0.

She had gotten one B in history class last year from Mr. Swasy, the most hated teacher at Bennett Elementary, and went ballistic. She demanded a parent conference and refused to accept the grade, claiming that Mr. Swasy hadn't calculated correctly. This led her to the principal's office, where she became even more belligerent until finally Swasy admitted that he had forgotten to add in her extra credit assignment on World War I and the impact it had on European children. The report had been twenty-two typed pages. How Swasy had forgotten about it baffled even George and Juan.

To go along with the brains, she had the looks. Like Juan, Samantha was dark-featured. Her tan skin and beautiful dark brown hair were an attractive combination. She was just as tall as Juan and George and equally strong. She had three older brothers, all of whom were much older and much bigger. She had gotten her toughness from being the smallest and, of course, the most picked on.

"So, what did Paul say?" George asked, motioning with his flashlight for Samantha to move along.

Samantha turned and continued down the cavern. "He told Laura that her front teeth were so big she could cut down the forest behind the school."

George and Juan suppressed a laugh. They had known Samantha long enough to know that if she heard either of them laughing about her friend, she'd just get angrier.

"Can you believe that? What a jerk. Then as he's going out of the room, he tells her that maybe if she put on enough lipstick, it might hide her fangs." Samantha was outraged. "Jerk!"

Juan turned and looked at George with an unmistakable grin, even in the shadowy light. George nodded and laughed silently.

"Hello? Did you hear me?" Samantha demanded, irked that neither George nor Juan had responded.

"How can we not? You're almost shouting," Juan said sardonically.

"Ah, boys," said Samantha in a disgusted tone. "What is it with guys? They think they're all that."

"Hey, don't put us in the same category as Paul," Juan piped up strongly. "We don't do stuff like that."

This seemed to settle Samantha a bit because she mumbled something to herself that sounded like "that's true" and walked on in silence.

The tube was growing smaller. Up ahead Samantha could see the crack that led to the larger area and Cavern L. She shuffled her feet slowly through the opening, turning her thin body so that she could get through more easily. Juan went next, having significantly more trouble but finally making it through, followed by George, who didn't have any problem.

"Keep it quiet," George whispered, shining his flashlight up at the ceiling of the cave. The ceiling was twenty-feet high and was decorated by slow growing stalactites. "If the bats are here, any noise will freak 'em out."

"Keep going," Samantha ordered, directing them forward toward a six-foot opening to their left. This was the entrance into Cavern L. It was the first of the three entrances, with U coming next, and finally C, even deeper into the cave.

Cavern L was like the rest of the cave: dark, wet, but easier to walk in, since the rough, sharp rocks of the tube were replaced by two inches of running water. The underground creek flowed over a level gravel bed for three hundred steps and then abruptly turned right.

Samantha had counted the steps once when she had forgotten to charge her flashlight batteries and the flashlight had gone out. Even though she had Juan and George with her at the time, she wanted to experience it without light, so the boys shut off their flashlights, and they all joined hands. Together, the three of them made their way to the corner of the L, some three hundred steps later.

It was around the corner that held their interest. Hundreds, if not thousands of bats lived inside the bottom portion of this particular cavern, and it was always an exhilarating feeling to shine a flashlight to the ceiling and see them hanging in massive clusters.

"Quiet," Samantha whispered, approaching the L.

The small creek pooled at the corner for a brief moment before slipping under an eroded lip in the facing wall. Samantha, George, and Juan worked their way around the bend and stepped up onto the path that led away from the creek into a damp, cavernous room. The ceiling was close to thirty-feet high and every inch of it was covered with black, winged objects.

"They're here," Juan whispered.

"Look at all of them," George said, keeping his voice hushed. "There's even more than before, I'll bet. What do you think, Samantha?"

Samantha didn't answer.

George took his eyes off the ceiling and shined his light into her face. "Samantha? What are you doing?"

But Samantha wasn't paying attention to George. In fact, she didn't hear his voice at all. Instead, her focus was on the object in front of her.

"What is that?" she whispered slowly, continuing to shine her light on it.

George traced her flashlight beam and stared.

"What are you guys doing?" Juan asked, adjusting his flashlight so that the light blended with the other beams. "What's that?"

Samantha stepped forward. "It looks like a . . . a . . . chest of some kind."

"A chest?" Juan mumbled, moving toward it.

Just as Samantha said, it was a chest, similar to a treasure chest. It was very large, made of wood and metal, with one large latch in the center and one smaller latch to the left and right. It looked old, battered, and weather-beaten. Juan drew closer and reached out to touch it, but Samantha shot out in a hoarse whisper: "Don't!"

"Why not?" Juan asked, looking at her curiously.

Samantha paused.

"Yeah, why not?" George said, stepping closer.

"I have a bad feeling about this," Samantha answered seriously. "What's an old treasure chest doing in the middle of a cave? Someone had to put that thing here, and recently. Think about it. We were here last weekend, but that Chest wasn't. Someone hid that Chest here, and they probably did it for a very specific reason, like to hide it. Whoever put that Chest down here doesn't want it to be found."

This made sense, George thought. "Not only that," he said, frowning, "but it looks heavy. Someone had to haul it down to this room."

"Whoa," Juan said, lifting his hand to his head. "I just thought of something. How did someone get that thing through the crack? There's no way it would fit. I can barely get through, and that's a lot wider than I am."

No one spoke as they kept their flashlights fixed on the Chest. It was nearly five minutes before Juan finally broke the silence. "We should get out of here."

"I agree," Samantha said, backing away.

But George stepped closer, now only a fingertip away from the latches.

"What are you doing?" Samantha demanded, still whispering. "You're not thinking about opening that, are you?"

George turned and smiled wryly at her. "Yeah, I am."

"Are you crazy?" Samantha blurted.

"Oh, come on. It can't be that bad. Maybe there's treasure inside."

"Or some body chopped up into pieces," Samantha retorted.

"Both of you keep your voices down. We'll have bats flying all over the place if you get any louder," scolded Juan in a harsh whisper. "And I don't think opening that thing is a good idea."

"Come on — it won't hurt to take a look."

George turned, and before Juan or Samantha could stop him, he unlatched the Chest and pushed the lid open. He bent over and shined his flashlight inside.

"Nothing," he whispered disappointedly.

"What?" Juan leaned forward to try and get a better look. "There's nothing inside. It's empty."

"Empty?" Samantha said in a shocked voice, wondering how that was possible since her imagination had convinced her that there was going to be a chopped up corpse inside.

Samantha and Juan shined their flashlights in, and just as George had said, the Chest was empty. In fact, it was clean and lined with a thick, white linen cloth, as though nothing had ever been put inside.

Samantha was about to go into how it was odd that an old-looking chest had such a new interior, but she didn't utter the words because what happened next changed her life, and the lives of her two friends, forever.

Chapter Two

The Chest of Light

Emerging like a charmed snake, a thin, white column of smoke filtered up and over the sides of the Chest. Samantha, George, and Juan could only stare as the cloud grew thicker and longer, hovering over the damp cavern floor.

"Wha — what's going on?" Samantha stammered. The cloud was growing larger and it wasn't long before the entire cavern was completely filled with it.

"I can't see," George said, groping blindly. "Juan, Samantha? Where are you?"

But there wasn't a response. Instead, they heard a thunderous voice echo from somewhere within the whiteness.

"TO YOU, THE GIFT OF FLIGHT," the deep voice rang out.

A beam of golden light pierced through the cloud of white gas and blasted toward George, striking him in the middle of his chest. The light wrapped around his upper body and he looked down in panic. It was as though the light was alive and dug into his coat before suddenly disappearing.

"TO YOU, THE GIFT OF INVISIBILITY," the deep voice bellowed.

A second beam of light pushed through the cloud and dug itself into Juan's chest. He screamed as the light wrapped around him for a moment and then vanished.

"TO YOU, THE GIFT OF KNOWLEDGE."

A third golden beam exploded into the air, heading directly into Samantha's chest. She, too, watched petrified as the light swam into her upper body and disappeared.

The thick gas was suddenly and abruptly sucked back into the open Chest as though it was being vacuumed up. When the last of the white mist had disappeared, the lid of the Chest flopped back down, the three latches snapped shut and in a blinding flash of golden light, it vanished.

What followed was absolute chaos. Hundreds upon hundreds of bats flew in every direction, smashing into the walls, and slamming into the spelunkers in complete confusion and disarray. Samantha fell to the ground and shrieked wildly, trying to pull the bats out of her long hair.

She rolled over and got to her feet. Bats everywhere, she moved forward toward the corner, to the pool of water. Holding the flashlight with her right hand, she flailed madly, trying to beat the crazed bats away.

SPLASH . . . into the small trickle of a creek. She was about to call for George and Juan, but something told her they were already ahead of her. She stumbled along blindly as the bats scattered everywhere.

She was almost to the edge and out of the water when she lost her balance and fell backward, her flashlight slipping out of her hands and tumbling under the shallow water. She could see its light being refracted as it skidded along the gravely bottom. She tried to get up, but lost her footing again, tumbling down in a somersault. She closed her eyes and banged her way along, reaching out for anything to grab and hold on to. Just as she was coming to a stop, she felt her legs being sucked down. Her body followed.

She had the sensation that she was shooting down, as though she was on a slide at a water park. She realized in that half second that she was in — as impossible as it seemed — a waterfall. She landed feet first, not that it helped much. The sudden jolt sent her to her knees as cold water poured over her neck and shoulders.

Samantha opened her eyes and immediately stared down at her chest. Glowing brightly with hundreds of miniature flashes of light was what looked like a vest. It was as though she was wearing a vest made of light, pure light, and it was illuminating everything around her. She could see her roughed up hands and the water splashing down around her. She put her hand to her chest and watched her fingers slip through the golden light as if it wasn't even there.

She got to her feet and moved out from under the waterfall. She looked up and watched as the falling water bounced off the cavern wall and plummeted down. She could barely make out the spot from where she had dropped some fifteen feet above.

"What happened?" she whispered to herself. "How did I end up here?"

Suddenly an answer shot into her mind, and she knew that she had fallen through an opening she never knew existed.

Samantha brought her attention to what lay ahead of her — a jagged mix of boulders and stones. Somehow she knew that she would have to navigate her way up through them, and if she did, she would be led out of the cave. But how did she know this? She had never been in this part of the grotto before, yet she was confident she knew exactly what she needed to do.

The first two boulders were relatively easy to get around, thanks in part to the light of the Vest; but the next ten were extremely difficult because the cavern was tight, and she was forced to climb vertically. She scaled boulder after boulder, squeezing over one and around another. Finally, after the twelfth boulder, she rested.

As she sat on the damp rock, her thoughts went to George and Juan. Were they all right? Were they lost? Again, something inside her was telling her they were fine; that they were worrying and searching for her. This was a comforting thought as she looked down at the sparkling Vest.

She pressed her hand into it and watched as the light moved and danced around her fingers, yet except for the fabric of her own drenched coat, she felt nothing. She turned her wrist and looked at her watch. Even though it was scratched from the fall, she could still make out the time.

Seven thirty.

How could it only be seven thirty? It seemed like it was the dead of night — like she'd been climbing for hours. She looked above her and knew that she had to continue. She stood up, stretched her arms over her head and kept climbing.

It wasn't long before a reddish glow from above caught her attention. She looked up and stared at maroon-colored clouds drifting lazily through the sky. Just seeing the sky and the freedom it represented invigorated her. She scaled the two remaining boulders quickly and stared at the circular opening in the ground above her. She bent down and with all of her energy leapt toward it. Her hands dug into the wet earth, and she hung on tightly, slowly pulling herself up. She reached for a small limb from an overhanging pine tree, which was all she needed to finally pull herself to freedom.

She let out a cry of relief and took in deep breaths while surveying the area around her. She was on a ridge and in front of her, about fifty feet away, was the ravine that she and her friends had followed to get to the cave. This meant, she thought as she made her way to the edge and looked over, that the entrance of the cave was now directly beneath her, far below.

Then something caught her eye — a movement below. She looked around feverishly and saw the red . . . the red from George's coat. He had made it out of the cave safely, just as she had sensed earlier. She cupped her hands around her mouth.

"George, George up here!" she shouted in elation. "I'm up here!"

George bolted out onto the trail and looked up at her. "Thank God!" he cried with relief. "We've been searchin' for you."

"I don't know how I'm going to get down. There isn't any trail."

"Hang on. I'll come get you."

She wondered if she had heard him correctly. How was he going to get up the enormous cliff? The question was answered almost immediately as she watched George ascend into the air, floating toward her as though he was standing on a magic carpet.

Samantha was dumbstruck. Within a few seconds, George was hovering magically in front of her. She stared incredulously and immediately noticed a sparkling, lighted Vest wrapped around his upper body — a Vest just like hers. Then she thought about her own Vest and looked down, but it was gone. The sparkling, flashing light had vanished, leaving only her soiled and torn brown coat.

"You look like crap," George said, continuing to float effortlessly.

"You're flying," Samantha managed to mumble, ignoring what she would have considered an insult any other time.

"Come on," George said, floating down so that he was touching the ground.

He held his arms out, and Samantha hugged him tightly, knowing what he was about to do.

"Here we go," he said, gently rising into the air.

"Oh, my . . ."

"Just hang on, Manthers," George said confidently as

he descended toward the trail. "Just a little longer. Juan's waiting for us."

Samantha looked down and saw the trail but didn't see Juan anywhere. George landed and Samantha pulled herself away, her mouth so wide open she could've swallowed a medium-sized frog.

"To you, the Gift of Flight," George said nonchalantly. "The Chest, remember? The light hit me and said I have the Gift of Flight. I can fly!"

"But . . ."

"The Vest," George said, pointing to the lighted Vest encircling his upper body. "It gives me the power to fly. It's incredible, but I know how to fly. I knew it as soon as the Vest formed."

"We're so glad you made it out okay," came Juan's voice from behind. Samantha wheeled around, but no one was there.

"I'm right in front of you."

Samantha stepped back and looked the trail over again. "Where are you?"

"You can't see me, can you?" Juan asked, with a twist of mischief in his voice.

"You're . . ."

"Invisible," Juan finished. "To you, the Gift of Invisibility."

"So you have a Vest around you, too?" Samantha asked, looking ahead of her where she assumed Juan was standing.

"Right," he answered.

Samantha sighed deeply. "What's happening?"

"We were given powers," George replied confidently, like he had known this was going to happen when he opened the Chest. "Didn't you get your Vest? The voice said that you had the Gift of . . ."

"Knowledge," Samantha said with a nod, her eyes closed. "Yes, I did. And now it makes sense. After I got hit with the light, I ran out of the cavern."

"I know, so did we," Juan mumbled from somewhere.

"But as I was going out, I slipped and fell and ended up in a completely different part of the cave. I lost my flashlight, but then the Vest was around me, and I could see clearly and I knew —" Samantha was rubbing her hands together and nodding, "I knew you guys were okay and that you were ahead of me. And I also knew that if I climbed over the boulders, the Vest would lead me to an opening."

"You see, you have the Gift of Knowledge, so you knew where to go."

"This is absolutely nuts," Samantha said incredulously.

"At least now I know why they call it Boulder Cave. I've never seen so many big rocks in one place."

George and Juan both laughed. Then, only a few feet in front of her, Juan became visible, as if he had popped out of the ground. He looked down at his chest but the Vest of Light that had covered his upper body and given him the power of invisibility had vanished. "Oh, no. It's gone. The Vest is gone!"

"And we can see you." George pointed out.

"Where'd it go? Where's the Vest?" he cried, dejectedly.

Samantha shrugged. "I don't know."

"George, you still have yours," said Juan, pointing at George's Vest.

"Yeah, I do," George exclaimed, looking down at the sparkling lights that glimmered and pulsed with bright white light.

"Oh, the time —" Juan suddenly remembered and looked at his watch. "Ten minutes to eight. We're gonna be late."

"My dad's gonna be mad," George grumbled. "Plus, he's gonna wonder what the heck happened to you, Samantha."

"What?" Samantha asked, a look of alarm crossing her face.

"Your face is all cut up, and your hair's all weird. You look like you got in a fight."

Samantha put her hands up to her hair, attempting to straighten out the chaos. "I'll just say I fell, which I did by the way, and that's why I look like this."

"Yeah, and why are you all wet? And what about your Vest, George?" Juan said, reminding him that he was still glowing. "How are you gonna explain that?"

George looked down at the sparkles. "I don't know."

"We've only got ten minutes, right?" Samantha asked, looking at her battered watch.

"Right," George answered.

"I'll bet if you fly us out of here, you can get us to Highway 97 in time."

"Hey, yeah. George, you can. You can fly us there," Juan added coaxingly.

George looked as though someone had hit him really hard in the face. "Are you sure? I don't know if I can."

"Lie down on the ground, and we'll climb on your back, like you're a horse," Samantha instructed.

"A horse?"

"Come on, just lie down," she pleaded.

George did as she asked, lying down on his stomach. Samantha climbed on and then Juan, both grabbing George's coat tightly.

"Ready, Juan?" Samantha asked.

"Ready."

"Let's go, George."

George lifted off the ground slowly, and both Samantha and Juan held their collective breath wondering if he could really take them on his back. George couldn't believe how easy it was. He figured the extra weight would make the flying more strenuous, but it didn't. His friends felt light, and carrying them along wasn't a problem.

George climbed higher, leaving the trail below — ten feet, then twenty . . . thirty feet above the trail. He soared in and out of tall, lumbering pines easily and fluidly, making it seem as though this was something he had done all his life.

The three were silent, watching the landscape pass below. They didn't know it, but this was just the beginning of some of the most incredible moments they'd ever experience.

Just as Samantha had thought, ten minutes was plenty of time to get to State Route 97. George dropped to the ground as the sound of traffic grew louder. He was thinking the same thing as Juan and Samantha — that he shouldn't come flying down on his father with his two best friends on his back. It was going to be difficult enough trying to explain the sparkling Vest. Flying around might send his dad into a panic.

Samantha and Juan hopped off, and George stood up, admiring his shining Vest. "You were right. Good call, Manthers," he said, as the three of them set off along the trail.

"What an afternoon," Juan said in an exhausted voice. "What are we going to tell our parents? That some magic chest shot out light, I turned invisible, and George flew us back? They're gonna think we're crazy."

George suddenly stopped and looked down at his chest. His Vest had vanished without warning, and all he could see was the red from his coat.

"It's gone," he whispered in surprise.

Juan and Samantha stopped and stared. "Went away, just like that," Samantha said, snapping her fingers.

"Do you think it will come back?" George asked, almost desperately.

"I really don't know. Maybe if I had mine, I'd be able to tell you. What'd you think, Juan?"

"I don't know," he answered, very unsure of himself. "I don't understand any of this. We find some chest in the middle of a cave that shoots out light and smoke, and then that voice shouting. Things like this don't happen. And what about that Chest? It just exploded into nothing. I have no idea about these Gifts, but when I was invisible, I felt so good. Everything looked like it does to me now, only you guys couldn't see me."

"That's right," George said.

"I want that power again," Juan continued. "I want to be able to turn invisible. Don't you want to be able to fly again, George?"

George nodded.

"And don't you want to be able to know more things?" Juan addressed Samantha, and she too, nodded in agreement.

"I do, too. How can we get the powers back?"

George had a theory and was about to tell Juan, but a familiar voice made him jump.

"George, let's go. Come on, it's time to go you guys!" his dad shouted from the base of the trail, walking slowly in their direction.

"Dad!" George called back in shock. "Ahh, we're coming."

"So, what are we going to do?" Samantha asked quickly and quietly, while the three of them walked very slowly down the trail toward Mr. Luisi.

"About what?" George asked in a whisper.

"About our parents? Are we going to tell them the truth?"

George and Juan looked at each other. Neither of them really knew what to do or what to say. Everything had happened so quickly and unbelievably, they didn't have time to ponder what they were going to do next.

"So, how was it?" George's dad greeted them with a smile as Samantha eyes darted to George's. It was decision time, and George cleared the large lump in his throat.

Chapter Three
The Blurry Shadow

George's father was an in-shape, forty-five year old. One could tell just by looking at him that he was fit. His arms were muscular and toned, and his thigh muscles bulged when he walked. What little hair he had on the sides of his head was shaved down almost to the skin. Although at first glance he looked rough and rather foreboding, he was really a gentle, kind man.

"Well," he said just as enthusiastically as he had the first time, "how was the cave?"

He grinned so wide Juan wondered if he could actually see all of Mr. Luisi's teeth. Mr. Luisi prided himself on his knowledge of Boulder Cave and asked questions every time about what they'd done and seen. Today, however, was not a day of welcomed questions about their experience.

"It . . . was . . . good," George stammered.

Juan thought that they were probably the most unnatural three words he had ever heard George speak in all the years he had known him. Mr. Luisi obviously picked up on it because his smile disappeared, and he a donned a more concerned look. Then his eyes surveyed Samantha, who looked like she'd gotten into a fight with a group of angry cats. As much as she smiled and tried to look normal, it was becoming apparent to Mr. Luisi that the trip into the cave had been anything but normal.

"What happened?" Mr. Luisi asked, his brow tightening. "Samantha, you look like you . . ."

"Fell," she said very quickly. "We were at Cavern L, and I was going along the creek bottom. . . ."

"The water got you, didn't it?" Mr. Luisi broke into a smile, putting everyone at ease for the moment.

"Yes," she replied brightly. "I lost my balance and tumbled down a ways."

"Luckily, you didn't hurt yourself any worse."

"Oh, it wasn't that bad of a fall, really," Samantha said, playing it down.

"Your mother won't like it," said Mr. Luisi with a sigh. "She's always telling me I shouldn't let you three go in there by yourselves. By the looks of you, Samantha, maybe she's right."

"Really, it wasn't that bad," Samantha insisted. "Besides, it was worth it. We saw the bats."

The smile returned. The bats were Mr. Luisi's favorite. "Ah, the bats. A lot of them, were there?"

"A ton, Dad. The whole ceiling was covered with them," George stepped in with a much more natural and fluent attempt than his last.

"I should've gone with you," Mr. Luisi sighed.

"Ah, no, I don't think you would've liked it much, Dad," George said quickly. "The bats were cool, but it was pretty much the same old thing."

"Still, there's something about that cave," Mr. Luisi said reflectively. "I've been in a lot of caves but Boulder has a certain power. It's hard to explain."

Juan, George, and Samantha stared at each other wide-eyed.

"I'll come with you next time. It's been too long since my last visit. C'mon, let's get back to the truck."

They followed Mr. Luisi down the remaining portion of the brush-laden trail to the large Suburban parked in a wide turnout on the shoulder of State Route 97. George lived twenty-five miles west of Wenatchee, the nearest city. Wenatchee, a word taken from the Native Americans inhabiting this area of Washington state, was the same name given to the meandering river that flowed nearby.

Living twenty miles out — away from the city and

the congestion had its advantages, and one of them, the one that Mr. Luisi liked best, was that he didn't have neighbors. George had lived along the Wenatchee River all his life. When people asked him about neighbors or friends to play with, he laughed. The nearest house was a mile east.

The farm, as his father called it, was a modest six-acre plot of land that sat uncultivated and, for the most part, untouched. Besides George's horse, Bluecher — which Juan liked to ride more than George did — and the fenced pasture, little about the place had changed for as long as George could remember. Most of the land was covered with tall pines, and a small brook cut a path through the north end. It was home to a variety of animals including deer, elk, raccoon, and George's semi-pet porcupine, Harold, who came around to the back deck every few nights to check for food George sometimes put out.

Thirty minutes later, Mr. Luisi pulled into his gravel driveway. Parked near the five-foot tamarack tree growing near the corner of the garage was a white station wagon which George immediately recognized as the one that Samantha's mother drove. Samantha's mom would be giving Juan a ride home because he lived fifteen miles east, back toward Wenatchee.

Juan lived on a ten-acre apple orchard that his parents had owned since he was four. His house was a three-bedroom rambler painted pearl white, and could just barely be seen from the highway. He liked where he lived and, just like George, didn't have the traditional neighbor close by. The nearest one was Patty Hazel, a pompous, extra skinny seventh-grader who went to the same middle school he did.

Samantha lived closest to the city in a white five-bedroom, two-story house on Deer Creek Road, just inside the city limits. Unlike Juan and George, Samantha's parents owned a very plain quarter-acre lot of land that they kept well manicured. Her neighborhood was more traditional. There were sidewalks, streetlights, and just about every house on Deer Creek had a two-car garage and a green front lawn or a basketball hoop. Unlike her two constant companions, Samantha had neighbors, but she wasn't interested in them. They were all boys and they were "immature" as she constantly told her mother.

The ride home had been silent as George, Juan, and Samantha tried to figure out what to tell their parents. Juan had the most time, since he would be the last to actually see his mom and dad, but Samantha and George had to be ready as soon as they got out.

Mr. Luisi led them up the cement walk to the wood deck where his wife and Mrs. Banks sat talking on white plastic lawn chairs. It was almost dark by now, but there was still enough light for Mrs. Banks to notice Samantha's abrasions, wild hair, and wet clothes.

"What happened to you?" she asked, standing up.

"Fell in L," Samantha said pleasantly, as if it had been just what she had wanted to do.

"What?"

"Lost her balance," Mr. Luisi added, putting his hand gently on Samantha's shoulder. "She fell in the little creek there by Cavern L. Nothing to worry about."

"Are you all right?"

"Fine," Samantha answered coolly.

"I still don't like them going in there by themselves," said Mrs. Banks pointedly as she looked at George's dad.

"I'm fine, Mom, really," Samantha said soothingly, hoping to defuse the hint of worry and distrust she could sense in her mother's voice.

"Still, you could've been hurt," Mrs. Banks barked, brushing her fingers through Samantha's long, tangled brown hair.

Mrs. Luisi shot a very deliberate, eyebrows-raised look at her husband as if to say, "I told you so."

"Oh, it's safe," Mr. Luisi said quickly. "I wouldn't let my own son go in there alone if I didn't think it was."

"I don't know," Mrs. Luisi piped up. "You've done your fair share of stupid things in your life, John, and I don't want these kids doing something that could put them in danger."

"Ah," Mr. Luisi grunted. He had heard this before. "If I thought George was in danger, I wouldn't let him go."

This upset his wife because her next sentence was higher in pitch and very forceful. "You said that the last time you let him go into that old missile silo near Vantage. Told me he was big enough and could handle it himself, but then after he got stuck . . . and the water . . ." Mrs. Luisi shuddered. "I hate to think what would've happened if you hadn't been there."

"Oh, Sophie," Mr. Luisi chuckled, "nothin' like that's gonna happen in Boulder Cave. The kids know every inch of it."

Samantha shot a scared look at George and Juan.

"Still!" Mrs. Luisi blasted. "Better safe than dead!"

"Right," said Mr. Luisi, rather quietly.

A strange silence followed, and George wondered if Mrs. Banks actually believed the lie when she said, very casually, "Well, you weren't hurt. C'mon, Juan, it's time to go. Thanks for the coffee, Sophie."

And Mrs. Banks led Juan and Samantha to the white station wagon and drove off. George watched Juan wave at him through the side window before the car cruised out of sight.

"Well, John," hissed Mrs. Luisi, "she could've been hurt. You and your obsession over that cave. I think these kids don't need to be going in there anymore, at least not without you."

Had his mother said this a week ago, George would've become very angry and argued with her, but considering what had happened just a couple of hours ago, he wasn't ever planning on going into Boulder Cave again, alone or with his dad.

Mr. Luisi nodded his head pensively, although George thought he was doing it so he wouldn't have to listen to another earful from his wife. George decided this was enough for him and made his way to the door, but stopped as his mother called him over.

"What?" he said.

"Is everything all right?" she asked, staring at him intently.

"Fine."

"Anything else happen in the cave you want to tell me about?"

George gulped. Why was she asking this? He looked down at his chest quickly to make sure that the Vest hadn't suddenly materialized, but the sparkling, flickering lights weren't there.

"Oh, Sophie, Samantha just tripped," Mr. Luisi said, exasperated. "Go on in, George. There's fried chicken and some potatoes in the oven."

"Okay," George said, turning toward the door.

"I made a fruit salad," his mother called as George stepped inside.

"Great," he said before shutting the door behind him.

George breathed a deep sigh of relief. He wasn't sure why, but telling his parents that some unknown Chest gave him the ability to fly didn't seem like the thing to do, at least not at this point.

Making his way to the kitchen, he passed through the living room where his younger sister sat on the couch, watching a television show intently.

"Hey," he said, walking past and turning to his left to go into the kitchen.

The kitchen was decorated with a dairy cow theme: Holstein cows were depicted playing carelessly around a farm on the wallpaper border; a cow-shaped tea kettle sat on the top of the old, missing-a-few-knobs stove; there was a bovine salt and pepper shaker and a napkin holder that looked like the cow had been vertically split in half.

Not that George cared about any of this. He didn't,

but he found it all somewhat ironic that the land, the farm, didn't have a single cow on it. Often, people would come over and ask his mother where the cows were simply because they assumed, based upon the kitchen, that she had somewhat of a dairy in the backyard. This wasn't true, of course. Mrs. Luisi had never milked a cow in her life.

George opened the oven and sure enough, there were three legs of crispy fried chicken and a shriveled baked potato. He took the warm plate out quickly and moved it over to the chipped kitchen table. He went to the refrigerator and pulled out the milk, pouring himself a large glass. He opened the drawer to the silverware and took a fork out before grabbing his glass of milk and returning to the kitchen table.

"How was the cave?" asked Dennis, coming in from another room as George sat down.

"Fine," replied George, taking a bite out of a chicken leg.

"It's good chicken," his younger brother said as he crossed the room to the refrigerator.

Dennis Luisi was a year younger than George, and although the two boys were close in age, they were very different. Dennis didn't like Boulder Cave much—he'd only gone with George twice. Unlike George, Dennis wasn't much of an explorer or risk taker. He was a calm, mild-tempered boy with an affection for books. He loved reading and collecting them. His room looked like a library with books on every topic. There were books he had bought at yard sales or school book fairs; donated books, and even a few textbooks from school he had forgotten to return, (and probably never paid for). Consequently, Dennis was smart as a whip. School came easy for him, even though he studied like it didn't, and his grades were always at the top of the class. While George considered himself to be just normal smart — where he should be for his age — he thought his brother was a genius.

Just last year for science fair, Dennis had created a project on cold fusion that had won him a trip to New York for a national competition where he placed third in his age group. George didn't even know what cold fusion was, and when his brother tried to explain it to him and how his project worked, George felt like his mind was melting down.

Dennis pulled out the milk, went to the cupboard, grabbed a bowl and proceeded to pour in Lucky Charms.

"See the bats?" he asked, getting a spoon from the drawer before sitting down at the table.

George was busy stuffing down a heap of potato and waited until he had swallowed most of it before answering. "Yeah, saw 'em," he replied casually.

"Don't you get sick of going in there?" Dennis asked in

wonder. He had never been able to figure out what George thought was so cool about the cave.

"No," George answered, at what he considered to be a very stupid question.

"I don't see what's so cool about it, I really don't. It's the same thing every time isn't it?"

For a brief moment George wanted to answer, "Oh, not today it wasn't," but he didn't. He just nodded and took another bite of potato.

The boys sat and ate in silence: George thinking about how he could possibly get his Vest back and the power of flight without anyone noticing, and Dennis trying to figure out why his computer wasn't accepting the extra hard drive he had installed earlier in the day. Their ten-year-old sister broke the silence.

"How's the cave?" Brenda asked, skipping into the kitchen.

"Fine," George said plainly.

"Bats?"

"Yeah."

"Cool," Brenda mumbled, rummaging through the cupboard looking for something sweet to eat.

Brenda was a skinny, long-haired ball of energy. She rarely sat unless it was in front of the television, and she often carried on conversations with people while doing something else at the same time. Some found this to be distracting, assuming that she wasn't paying attention, but that was an illusion. Brenda was a listener, even though she didn't look at you when you spoke.

"See ya," she said, shutting the cupboard and heading back to the living room with a Hershey bar in her hand.

"Mom better not see you with that," warned Dennis as she walked by.

"See you with what?" came their mother's voice just before her pudgy body rounded the corner and stopped in front of Brenda, who was trying to conceal the candy bar behind her back.

"Nothing," Brenda said uncomfortably.

George cracked a smile as he got up from the table. Brenda never lied very well. As she stood there, her cheeks began to turn tomato red.

"Give it up," Mrs. Luisi said, her hand outstretched.

"But Mom, it's only a Hershey."

"Now. I don't want you having a candy bar this late. Hand it over."

Brenda slapped the bar into her mom's hand.

"Thank you. You can have some yogurt if you want."

Brenda thought about it, shook her head, and moped

around her mother and back to the living room.

"Good chicken, Mom," George said, dumping the bones in the garbage and scraping his plate clean.

"Just put the plate in the sink with the rest of the dishes," she called as Dennis got up from the table.

"I'm gonna shower and go to bed," George told her, now feeling quite sleepy with a stomach full of warm food.

"Okay," his mother said, turning her head slightly and shouting at her daughter, "It's almost time for bed, Brenda. It's a school night."

"Tired?" Dennis asked, following George out of the kitchen and down the hall toward their bedrooms.

"Yeah, long day," George sighed, again trying to sound as natural as possible.

"Well, I'm gonna go back in and try to figure this computer out," Dennis said, opening his bedroom door. "Good night."

"Night."

By the time George had showered, brushed his teeth, and climbed into bed, he was exhausted, more mentally than physically. Ever since arriving home, he had been replaying what happened in Boulder Cave over and over again in his mind. The white mist, the thundering voice, and his ability to fly . . . it was just too incredible to fathom. Who would believe such an outrageous story?

Having replayed the scenes to no end, he finally drifted into sleep. This was little relief as his dreams were wild spin-offs from the events of the day. In one scene, he had flown so high he'd gone into space and saw what he thought looked like some sort of lighthouse with giant knights guarding two large, golden doors. But it was the dream that he gotten trapped under a pile of fallen rock as Boulder Cave collapsed that had awakened him. As he opened his eyes, he knew immediately from the illuminated room that the Vest of Light had returned.

He sat up and pushed the covers away. And there it was. A Vest of sparkling, golden light linked together around his upper body like a piece of clothing. He looked over at the digital clock, which read two a.m. in glowing red numbers. He turned his attention to his bedroom window. The light from the full moon was bright, and he was quickly out of his bed, his face pressed against the glass.

The landscape had a silver glow to it, and he could see everything easily. Then the thought struck him. He stripped off his pajamas and went to the closet grabbing a thick sweater and a pair of sweats from his dresser. He looked down at the sparkling Vest and then pulled the sweater over his head. For a brief moment the Vest disappeared but then emerged through the sweater and continued glowing. He marveled at this for a time before getting the rest of his clothes. In just a couple of minutes he was fully dressed, quite warmly, and ready. He slid the window open slowly and as silently as possible.

It was quiet and the evening was warm. He jumped out of the window, and instead of landing on the ground only a few feet below, he soared up into the air and over his house. The feeling was incredible. Never in his life had he felt so free and so powerful, and yet it was all so effortless.

He hovered fifty feet above the house and surveyed the land. He was vertical, as though he was able to stand atop the air itself. But how was he flying? He wasn't moving any part of his body, yet it was like his mind was controlling his movements without him having to think about it.

He shifted from a vertical to a prone position, his arms extended out in front of him. He soared forward for a few feet, then slid smoothly to his left. He moved higher, gliding over two large pine trees that bordered the creek.

Fists clenched and arms out, he tore off into the air, accelerating so fast that the wind raked his face like tiny spikes. The landscape below was a blur, and he found himself high above the Wenatchee River when he finally came to a stop.

He stared at the river, watching the water rumble over the tall boulders. George was as happy as he had ever been in his life. Nothing had ever felt better. The sheer ability to take flight so effortlessly was something he never wanted to lose.

He was about to descend closer to the river when something along the dike caught his eye. He watched as it moved along, going so fast it was a blur of shadow. The object, whatever it was, was traveling at tremendous speed.

George followed it with his eyes and watched as it turned abruptly left, heading along the dirt trail that led from the river to his house. He sped forward still high above and chased it, trying to keep up but it was useless. By the time he was hovering over his house, the speeding object had vanished.

George stared nervously. What had that thing been? An animal? No, that wasn't possible. Animals couldn't move so fast that they turned into a blur. What could possibly travel at such an incredible rate of speed?

George wiped the tears from his eyes that had formed from the short blast of acceleration and continued his scan. Ten minutes passed, and the speeding object wasn't anywhere around. He wasn't sure what it was, but he knew he hadn't imagined it.

He turned, flew back to the dike, and landed where he had seen the object. The dirt was dry and coarse, and maybe, just maybe . . .

He bent down and traced the shape in the dirt with his finger. Then he looked forward, and there they were: freshly made imprints in the dirt tracing the exact path in which the something had gone.

The hair on the back of his neck stood on end, and a cold, eerie feeling made his stomach tighten. That blurry thing had been human, George thought as he stared at the row of footprints made by a pair of very large tennis shoes.

Chapter Four
Mr. Dorn's Class

Samantha was wearing jeans, a gray, long-sleeve sweater, and a pair of white Nikes. She stood next to the stop sign at the corner, her backpack slung across her shoulder. According to her watch, it was seven forty-five and sure enough the bus bearing the name Eagle Crest approached slowly, finally rolling to a stop as the red STOP sign swung out to halt traffic.

"Hi, Mr. Ivan," she said, climbing aboard.

"Hello, Samantha," the sixty-year-old bus driver said kindly. "You look nice today."

Samantha smiled as she walked past him, looking around the full bus until she found Kristina, one of her good friends from Bennet Elementary where she'd had gone to school last year.

Kristina scooted over next to the window so that Samantha could sit down next to her.

"Hi," Kristina said.

"Hi, Kris," said Samantha cheerfully. "What'd you do this weekend?"

The bus started up again, and the loud engine noise made it necessary to practically shout to be heard.

"I went to the fair with my mom," Kristina said with a hint of disappointment in her voice. "It was fun, but I hate that stupid ring toss booth."

"What about it?"

"You know which one I mean?"

Samantha nodded. "The one with the big stuffed animals. Yeah, I know the one you're talking about. I never win at that one. I swear it's impossible."

"Exactly. I spent fifteen bucks at that booth and I could never get all three rings around the bottles," Kristina said, annoyed. "I just want the big pink elephant they have sitting above all the other stuffed toys. Every year I try for it. You know, I've never even seen anyone win at that booth."

"Neither have I."

"Hey, Samantha," a voice from the very back of the bus called above the noise. Samantha scowled. The voice belonged to Paul Hertzinger, the biggest moron in the entire sixth grade, (according to Samantha). She, along with most of the girls at Eagle Crest Middle School, loathed him.

"I hate him," Samantha hissed through clenched

teeth.

"Who doesn't? He thinks he's so cool. He goes around hitting people and swearing all the time." Kristina disliked him as much as Samantha did.

There was stirring behind the two girls as people grunted and whispered things like, "Jerk," "Get off me," "Watch it." Kristina was about to ask Samantha what her weekend consisted of when Paul poked his face between them from behind.

"Ladies," he said smoothly, "how are we today?"

"We," Kristina said sharply, "don't like you!"

"Oh, come on now, Krissy. Everyone knows I'm the best looking dude in school."

Samantha gave a hearty laugh. "Yeah, right."

"You know the fall dance is coming up, and I was wondering if either of you, well, if both of you would like to go with me."

Samantha was so shocked she couldn't laugh. What could possibly make him think she liked him? Kristina wasn't holding back.

"Listen, you fat wart, I wouldn't go with you to the dance. Do you think I like you?"

Paul went very red but moved his eyes to Samantha. For a brief moment she felt pity for him, but then remembered how he'd made fun of Laura Powell's teeth. That did it.

"Forget it, Paul," she snapped, aggravated at herself for ever feeling the teeniest bit sorry for the loser.

As Paul scooted away, he mumbled an obscenity that made Samantha glare back at him as he rejoined his friends in the back seat.

"What a jerk! I hope no one says yes to him," Samantha said angrily.

Kristina grunted. "Oh, right. You know that Missy Jenkins will go. She's the biggest flirt in school."

"Yeah, probably."

Fifteen minutes later the bus pulled up in the front of the school and students got off, scattering in various directions like misplaced ants. Samantha arrived about ten minutes before classes started and wanted to find George or Juan before first period. She knew if she found one, she would find the other. She couldn't remember a time when they weren't together.

She said good-bye to Kristina and headed down the hallway in the opposite direction. She wove in and out of people, saying "Hi" and smiling at friends while keeping an eye out for Juan and George. At the end of the long hallway, she spotted them talking beside the locker they shared.

"Hey, Samantha," Juan said, waving her over. "George was just telling me about . . ." Juan looked around to be sure no one could hear him, ". . . what happened last night."

"Why are you whispering?"

"Because," Juan snapped, still in a whisper, "he got his Vest last night."

Samantha's mouth dropped open.

"Yeah, that's what Juan looked like," George laughed.

"Go on, tell her, George. Tell her from the beginning," Juan begged.

"What?" Samantha asked, now whispering.

"I had a dream last night about a lot of weird stuff, and all of it had to do with the Vest. In one of my dreams, I saw a lighthouse in space. The earth was far below it, and there were these guards, these huge knight-like guards at the front of two massive, golden doors that led inside."

"Really?" Samantha was intrigued.

"But that one went away, and I had another dream where I got trapped underneath a pile of fallen rock from Boulder Cave. That's when I woke up, and when I did," George said excitedly, "I had my Vest, so I got dressed and flew out my bedroom window."

"What?" Samantha asked. "Are you crazy? What if someone saw you?"

"Where I live? At two o'clock in the morning? Come on."

"True," Samantha agreed.

"The moon was full, and I could see everywhere so I flew all around, you know . . . practicing. I went high over the river, and that's when I saw it."

"Saw what? Come on, tell me!"

"That's the thing, because I'm not sure what I saw. The movement caught the corner of my eye, and I followed it."

"Followed what?"

"Well, it was like a blur, really."

"Huh?" Samantha looked bewildered.

"It was a blurry shadow, and it was going fast. I mean so fast that whatever it was turned into a blur. It went along the top of the dike and then toward my house," George whispered.

"You were dreaming," Samantha said, dismissively.

"No, I wasn't!" George said more loudly than he intended. Quickly looking around to see if anyone else heard, he lowered his voice before continuing. "I chased it for awhile but it was too fast and got away. I went back to the dike and looked at the dirt. There were fresh footprints made by tennis shoes, about a size twelve, I'm guessing. My dad wears a twelve, and they looked about his size."

"Maybe they were your dad's," Samantha suggested.

"My dad with a pair of tennis shoes? On the dike? My dad never wears tennis shoes. He's always got boots on. Anyway, these prints were fresh."

"What are you saying?" Juan tried to piece it together. "That a human ran so fast he turned into a blur?"

George threw up his hands for a moment. "I don't know what I'm saying. I'm just telling you I saw something last night that was really weird. There was something about that thing or person or whatever it was, that made me shiver."

Neither Juan nor Samantha said anything more as the bell rang, signaling that class was starting in two minutes.

"We better get going. Let's talk at lunch," Juan said quickly.

"Okay," replied George, watching as Juan made his way down the hallway with the hundreds of other students.

Samantha and George walked in the opposite direction to Mr. Dorn's mathematics class in Room 213. Mr. Dorn was a tall, white-haired man who looked like he was too old to be teaching.

"And you have no idea what the blur really was?" Samantha asked, picking up the conversation where it left off.

"No, but it was creepy."

They slowly made their way up the crowded staircase

and down the hall, finally reaching Mr. Dorn's room. George waited for Samantha to enter and then followed. She sat on the left side of the square room and George on the exact opposite, parallel with her.

Mr. Dorn was standing at the front of the class, his small hazel eyes hiding behind a pair of thick round spectacles. The last few students straggled in and took their seats just as the tardy bell rang.

The first five minutes of Mr. Dorn's class were utterly useless. Everyday he read each name from the class roster in alphabetical order in his slow drawl.

"Armstrong . . . Natalie."

"Here."

"Baily, Gerald."

"Here."

"Banks, Samantha."

But before she could respond, Tom Chan, one of Paul's cronies who sat two seats to her left, said loudly, ". . . is an idiot," causing the class to erupt in laughter. Samantha turned and glared at him, feeling her cheeks go hot and red.

"Mr. Chan," came Mr. Dorn's slow voice, "I don't appreciate that comment. Please keep quiet."

It didn't surprise Samantha that Mr. Dorn knew Tom's name. He was making cracks like that all the time, but she wanted a little more reprimand than the weak effort offered up by Dorn. Tom ranked high on Samantha's people-I-don't-really-like list, right up there with Paul Hertzinger.

But Mr. Dorn simply continued his exhaustive attendance check-in.

"Carney, Frank."

"Here."

And on and on it went until finally — about five minutes later — Mr. Dorn reached Junior Zanol, the last name of the roster.

"Today," Mr. Dorn said, looking up at the class, "we will be studying the use of negative numbers."

Noticing a light flicker below her, Samantha looked down at her shirt and stared as little balls of light began bouncing wildly all over in the shape of a brightly lit Vest covering her upper body. She looked up in panic and stared at George, but he wasn't looking at her. He was looking at Mr. Dorn, as unbelievable as that seemed because George never paid attention to Dorn's lessons. She looked down again and the Vest was glowing even brighter. She stared around frantically at everyone else. How was she going to explain this?

She wasn't sure why she stood up suddenly in the middle of the class, but without realizing what she was doing, she found herself standing beside her desk.

"Miss Banks," said Mr. Dorn irritably. "What are you doing?"

Samantha stood there, wide-eyed, looking around as if she had just entered a room full of aliens.

"Miss Banks," stormed Mr. Dorn, "is there a problem?"

"No," she said meekly.

"Then I would appreciate it if you sat down. Unless, of course, you feel like you don't need to learn the basics of algebra and negative numbers."

Then an answer shot out of her mouth that shocked everyone in the room, including her. "I already know everything about negative numbers."

The class laughed, but stopped when Mr. Dorn put up a hand. "Excuse me?"

Samantha, still standing, still wearing a brilliant, glowing Vest of light, said again, incredulously, "I already know everything about negative numbers, and I really don't see why I have to learn about them all over again."

George was absolutely stunned. As if the glowing Vest wasn't enough, Samantha never, ever talked to teachers in that tone, in that I-know-more-than-you sort of voice, and even Samantha herself was surprised that she had blurted out her thoughts so openly. But part of her, a large part of her, believed that Mr. Dorn needed to hear it.

The teacher looked furious. George thought he might suddenly explode, he had turned so red. Mr. Dorn moved to the board, mumbling incoherently, but George managed to hear something along the lines of, "Think you know it all, do you? Young people. Thinks she's so smart."

He wrote three problems on the board, and as soon as he had completed them and was about to ask Samantha what the answers were, she rattled the answers off so fast the old teacher looked as though he'd been slapped in the face.

"Negative seven, positive one, and positive six," Samantha whipped.

The classroom was silent. It was a very strange silence; a combination of disbelief and suspense, leaving the ball in Dorn's court because he knew, just as Samantha did, that her answers were correct.

"What happens when two positives are multiplied together?"

"Nothing. The answer remains positive. Was that a trick question?" Samantha cocked her head to the side like a curious puppy. "You were trying to get me to say negative? The only time you see a change like that in multiplication is when you have two negatives multiplied together. When that happens, the two numbers form a positive."

Mr. Dorn was fuming. He shook his head and rifled

through to the back of his teacher's edition. He took the book and wrote a complex problem on the board that, to George, looked like a bunch of letters and numbers all thrown together with a few sets of parenthesis. He had never seen a problem like the one Dorn was scribbling. It took the teacher a few moments to finally complete writing the equation on the white board, and before he could even ask, Samantha answered.

"X is equal to negative two sevenths," she said coolly.

Mr. Dorn stared at her, anger shooting from his eyes. The fact that she had given the correct answer so quickly added fuel to an already burning fire. If he had been calmer, he might have marveled at the fact that she figured out the answer to such a difficult problem so quickly.

"Miss Banks," the teacher spat, "you are a very rude young lady. I do not appreciate . . ."

But, unbelievably, Samantha cut him off. "Was my answer correct?"

This took Mr. Dorn aback. "What?"

"My answer, was it correct?"

"That's hardly the point. You . . ."

"That is the point. It's math class. Is that the correct answer?" Samantha repeated strongly, her Vest beaming.

"I said . . ."

"IS THAT THE RIGHT ANSWER?"

Before Mr. Dorn had a chance to erupt, George jumped up from his desk and shouted as loudly as he could: "FIRE!"

The eyes of the class shifted from the front of the room to George, who was now hopping up and down, screaming like a crazed fool.

"What are you doing?" shouted Dorn.

"FIRE!"

"What are you talking about?"

"In my shoe, there's a fire in my shoe!"

The class burst out in hysterics, and this was the final straw. Mr. Dorn looked like a raving maniac. He charged over to George and shouted at him to sit down so loudly that George's ears rang. But George didn't sit down. Instead, he continued hopping like a complete idiot.

"YOU WILL GO DOWN TO THE OFFICE!" Dorn bellowed, and then his eyes shot over to Samantha. "YOU TOO!"

The classroom went silent again.

"GO . . . NOW!"

"What did I do?" Samantha asked innocently.

"MISS BANKS, GET OUT OF MY CLASSROOM!"

And with this, she and George grabbed their backpacks and went to the door at the back of the room. Samantha's

Vest was glowing brightly, and before she left the class, she turned and looked at the red-faced, bloodshot Dorn.

"That was the right answer," she said proudly.

"GET OUT!"

Samantha slammed the door and looked at George, who stared at her in utter astonishment.

"What was that?"

"Me?" Samantha laughed, pointing at him. "What about you, shouting 'fire' and jumping up and down like a moron?"

"I was trying to distract Dorn. He was about to explode, he was so mad, and you kept standing there whipping out answers. What got into you?"

"I don't know," Samantha said quietly as they stood in the empty hallway. "I don't know why I just did what I did."

George shook his head. "Everyone saw your Vest. Now everyone's gonna know."

Samantha started down the hallway, looking at the row of lockers with sudden interest. "George," she said as he followed next to her.

"What?"

"We're the only ones who can see the Vests."

George stopped and grabbed her wrist. "What do you

mean?"

"No one in class saw my Vest except you," Samantha said seriously. "Me, you, and Juan are the only ones who can see the Vests."

"You're sure?"

"Positive. My Vest told me."

George let go of her wrist and rubbed his hands together. "Amazing. But the Vests give off light. People must be able to see that."

Samantha shook her head. "They can't."

George stared at her Vest shining brilliantly over her shirt. It sparkled and danced with novas of light all across her chest and shoulders. "The Vest of Knowledge. So, you know stuff," he said when the realization hit him.

"Yeah," Samantha replied casually, as if the Vest was an everyday occurrence.

"Tell me something."

"About what?" asked Samantha, now grinning.

"Anything. Hmm, tell me about . . ."

But George stopped because coming around the corner, looking very smug was Paul Hertzinger.

"Samantha," Paul said slickly, walking up to her flashing his missing-a-front-tooth smile. "Have you reconsidered about the dance?"

He was now face to face with her. Paul was a chubby, freckle-faced bully most sixth-graders feared. It was generally believed that Paul wasn't in school for an education, but to make everyone else's life miserable. His beady eyes glared at Samantha from underneath his thin, almost peanut-shaped eyebrows. His brown hair was uncombed and ran wild over his forehead and face, and he brought his hand up to brush his bangs out of his eyes.

"I've already told you. Are you that dense?"

"Oh, come on," Paul pleaded, stepping forward, puckering up in an attempt to kiss her.

"Hey, back off," George said, pushing Paul back.

"I see. You two are going out, are you?"

George rolled his eyes. "You're such a fool. You don't know anything about us. You ARE stupid."

Saying this seemed to trigger something because before he could defend himself, Paul had hurled his body into George, and the two boys skidded across the tiled floor.

Samantha watched as they tugged and pulled at each other, rolling around the middle of the silent hallway. She seemed frozen. It wasn't until Paul, who was now on top of George, began pulling at her friend's ear that she acted. George swore loudly and went for Paul's face with his hand, but pulled away as he saw Samantha raise her leg and swing her foot in a soccer-like movement right into the side of Paul's jaw.

She kicked him so hard that he tumbled off George and slid a few feet across the hall on his stomach. George got to his feet and stood next to her, watching as Paul struggled to get up, blood trickling out of his nose.

Just then, Mr. Spencer came bolting out of his class-room right next to where Paul and George had been fighting.

"What's going on here?" his voice cracked with anger as he rushed up to them.

Another classroom door flung open, and Mrs. Diggins, one of the science teachers, burst onto the scene.

"George started a fight with me," Paul lied, rubbing his jaw where Samantha had kicked him.

Mr. Spencer eyed George and Samantha and then glared at Paul suspiciously. "George started a fight with you?" he asked, almost sarcastically.

"Yeah, he called me a . . ."

"Save it!" Mr. Spencer stuck out his hand.

"That's not true," George spoke up. "He was . . ."

But Mr. Spencer's hand was now pointing at George, silencing him. "All of you down to the office," he said sternly.

"Where they should have been in the first place," came the slow, monotonic voice of Mr. Dorn, who had come out of his classroom in time to hear Paul claim it was George who had started the fight.

"I sent Samantha and George down to the office for inappropriate behavior but apparently they didn't think they were in enough trouble since they're fighting in the hallway. If you don't mind, Mr. Spencer, I will escort them to the office and explain to the principal what happened myself."

"Fine," Mr. Spencer said returning to his classroom. Mrs. Diggins looked outraged but also made her way back to her room, leaving Samantha, George, and Paul alone with Mr. Dorn who walked slowly toward the three of them.

"So mad you had to go and pick a fight, Luisi?"

"I didn't pick a fight!" George shouted. "Paul attacked me."

Paul gave a hearty laugh. "Yeah, right. I didn't touch him. I was walking down the hall, and Luisi just pushed me into the lockers for no reason."

"You liar!" Samantha shouted indignantly. "You were trying to kiss me, and then George stepped in and pushed you back. That's the truth, Mr. Dorn. I swear it."

Mr. Dorn glared at her. "We'll see what the truth is. Let's go."

Chapter Five
The Locker Room

PE with Mrs. Rossin was difficult, to say the least. For most students, PE meant fun activities and games, a means of taking one's mind off the dull lecture classes, like Mrs. Tuttle's world history class or Mr. Vale's English class. But for students in Mrs. Rossin's class, PE meant running and exercising, "not foolish games" as Mrs. Rossin often said. Juan figured that she might as well call the class PI, for physical insanity, because the forty-something teacher seemed every bit as insane as Juan's mental second cousin from Indiana who thought he was Santa Claus.

"Today," Mrs. Rossin said, sweeping into the gym where thirty students waited to hear the instructions of the day, "we will be doing corner relays."

There was a very audible groan from the majority of the students, but it was ignored by Mrs. Rossin as she continued. "Today's drill will be different. There will be throwers as well as runners."

She took two foam balls from the ball bag on the hardwood floor and held them as she continued her explanation. "There will be one line in each corner of the gym. Your goal is to get from one corner diagonally across the gym to the other corner without being hit with the foam balls. There will be two throwers and two retrievers. The throwers will have to stay inside the middle circle," Mrs. Rossin pointed to the blue circle in the center of the gym, "and the retrievers are to go and get the balls and bring them back to the throwers. If you get hit with the foam ball, you're out. The winning team is the line that has the most players left when I blow the whistle. Any questions?"

Lori Tilip raised her hand.

"Yes, Lori?"

"Do we have a time limit to get across the gym?"

"Yes. You must make it to the other side within seven seconds. Gregory," Mrs. Rossin pointed to the boy seated in the first row of the bleachers wearing a cast on his leg, "will be doing the counting. He will say 'Go,' and then count down from seven. If he gets to zero and you're still trying to get across, you're out. The next person in line does not go until Gregory has shouted 'Go' and has started counting again. If you make it successfully across, you are to continue standing; but if you're hit, you must go to the bleachers and sit.

Are there any more questions?"

There were a few murmurs, but no one raised their hand. "Good. I will number you by fours . . ." and she began sending people off to the corners until the entire class had either been sorted into runners, throwers, or retrievers.

Juan was in line three which meant he would be running diagonally across to line one. He was excited since this was the first time this year Mrs. Rossin had skipped the thirty-lap warm-up run and the vigorous fifteen-minute aerobic workout she normally used to start the class. In fact, the class hadn't even stretched, not that Juan minded. Any game that actually looked like fun was a welcome change.

Gregory shouted, "Go!" and the first people from each of the four lines charged across the gym as two throwers, each with two foam balls in their hands, waited.

Jenny Hearth, a tall, black-haired, tan-skinned girl had been the first one in Juan's line. She ducked under the first throw, but as Gregory shouted "Three" she was hit in the leg, and moved across to the bleachers with Luis Sternburg, a boy from line two who had also been hit.

Juan was the last one in his line. He watched as Alicia Garrett tried to cross the gym but was pelted in the forehead by Josh Zimmerman, a husky boy who Juan thought ought to try out for baseball because of the way he threw. Even though the ball was foam, it almost knocked Alicia to the ground, causing Mrs. Rossin to yell, "Don't aim for the head, Zimmerman!"

If someone had walked into the gym at that moment, they would've wondered if Mrs. Rossin had lost complete control of her class. Kids were running around the gym, laughing and shouting, some of them gathering balls, others trying desperately to duck and find their way to the other side, while still others sat complacently on the bleachers waiting for the game to end.

Juan thought that Doug Rondo had made it across safely, but just as the tall Black boy was about to cross the line, he was tagged in the back of the knee by one of Josh's super-throws.

"Dang," Doug shouted, clapping his hands together.

"Gotcha!" Zimmerman shouted at him.

"You got lucky, Josh."

Juan was growing anxious. The only person that had made it safely across was Enrique Rodgers, and that had been blind luck since Enrique was about as slow as a slug on a cold day. Juan stepped forward and waited until Gregory shouted, "Go!" and then took off. He sprinted diagonally across the floor as fast as he could, watching as Josh reared back to throw — but amazingly, Josh went for Vanessa Knight on the other side of the gym, and Juan headed home free.

"Made it," he said quietly to himself. He turned and walked toward Enrique, who was standing patiently on the baseline.

"Good job, Enrique," Juan said, congratulating him.

Enrique looked back and stared at Juan strangely and then turned his head left and right, as though . . . as though he couldn't see him.

"Who said . . ." Enrique's voice quivered.

Juan immediately knew what was happening. He looked down at his chest and sure enough, the Vest was glowing brightly around his upper body.

Enrique turned his attention back to Mrs. Rossin.

Juan stood there, rooted to the floor. He was invisible in the middle of PE class! But when had he turned invisible? Surely someone saw him. He looked around at the faces on the bleachers, but everything seemed normal. Some students looked disappointed, but no one looked surprised. Had he turned invisible while he was in line? Is that why Josh didn't go for him?

Juan moved to the back wall of the gym and slowly sat down. He watched dazed as the remaining players finished the game. Mrs. Rossin blew her whistle, and the class was sorted again into different positions. Suddenly, she began looking around the room as though she had lost something.

"Where is Ramirez?" she shouted, annoyed.

"Don't know," Enrique replied. "He was here just a few minutes ago."

"Go check the boys' locker room," she ordered, and Enrique went running off.

Juan stood up and wiped his sweaty hands on the sides of his shorts. What was he going to do? What if his Vest went away like the last time and he just sort of reappeared. What a scene that would cause. He didn't even want to think about the questions that would be asked.

Juan sprinted toward the boys' locker room door and stood still, waiting for Enrique to come back so he could slip in. Juan heard Gregory shout, "Go!" and the noise erupted again. Enrique threw the door open and ran onto the court toward Mrs. Rossin, shaking his head as he approached her.

Juan moved around the end of the door and slid silently into the locker room. He walked around the corner and stopped, listening hard and looking everywhere to make sure the locker room was empty. It was.

He took a great breath of air and sat down on a bench staring at his Vest. Of all the times to get it, right in the middle of PE. What luck. How had the Vest appeared? He hadn't said any special word or thought anything specific.

"Wait," he whispered. He did have the thought as he was standing in line that it would've been cool to be invisible so that he could get across the gym without being seen, but that was just a fleeting thought. Could that have caused his Vest to appear, merely by thinking about it?

He rubbed his dimpled chin. If he could think it on, maybe he could think it off. He closed his eyes and whispered, "Go off. Go off." He did this for more than a minute and then opened his eyes. The Vest was as bright as ever with brilliant flashes exploding in all directions like fireworks across his chest.

For the next forty minutes all Juan did was try not to think about his Vest, but it was useless. He was invisible, and there was nothing he could do to change that. Then he heard a rumbling noise growing closer. It was the class being dismissed to the locker room. Hearing the door swing open, he shot up from the bench, darted into the first toilet stall, and sat down.

Why had he just run? It wasn't like the other boys could see him. He realized in his haste that he hadn't closed the stall door all the way and got up to shut it when someone started pushing the door open. It was Josh Zimmerman.

Juan drew back to the seat and stared wildly. Zimmerman was using the stall Juan was in! He shut the door and began to take down his shorts and underwear. Juan did the first thing that came to mind. He yelled. But what came out was an animal-like screech.

Zimmerman was so frightened, he nearly fell over. He fumbled for the door handle while at the same time trying to pull up his shorts.

"What the . . ." he shouted, finally managing to get the door open.

"What was that?" came a boy's voice from nearby.

"Something's in there," Zimmerman screamed, pointing at the stall. "Did you hear it? It was in the stall."

By now a crowd of boys had gathered around Zimmerman, staring at the stall like it was some sort of possessed monster. Juan got to his feet and slid out silently.

"What happened?" one of the boys asked Zimmerman again.

"I don't know. I was getting ready to sit down to go and then I heard that friggin' scream."

"I heard it, too," said a red-haired boy stepping forward toward the stall.

"What are you doing?" Zimmerman asked in horror. "That's a ghost, man. I know it. It was like the thing was right behind me."

Juan couldn't believe what he was seeing. They hadn't

a clue that he was Zimmerman's supposed ghost. As he ambled along the wall, avoiding everyone, he couldn't help but smile a bit. It really was rather funny. Then he stopped, his eyes sparkling with a glint of mischief. Just about everyone's attention was on Zimmerman and the haunted stall, and Juan couldn't resist the opportunity. He checked to make sure his Vest was still on and then cupped his hands over his mouth, making the same strange noise he had before, only this time it was louder.

The entire locker room went crazy. Boys were scurrying back into the gym so fast it looked worse than an unpracticed fire drill. In less than a minute the whole locker room was empty, and Juan was laughing, holding his hand over his mouth. If only he'd had a camera.

Juan quieted down and listened. He could hear a low, deep voice bellowing and then heard the door blast open and watched as Mr. Shields strode into the room, followed reluctantly by the rest of the boys.

"What are you talking about?" Mr. Shields shouted in his military-like tone. "Get changed. You're going to be late for your next class. I don't have time for this."

"But Mr. Shields . . ." Zimmerman started weakly.

"Call me 'sir,'" Shields roared.

Sergeant Shields, (what he called himself) was a retired,

twenty-year Army veteran who had served as a drill sergeant before coming to teach eighth-grade PE. He was six-foot eight-inches tall, weighed about three hundred pounds, and looked so mean that Juan thought he could actually turn people into stone, like Medusa, if he wanted. His big, dark eyes surveyed the locker room. It was as quiet as Juan had ever heard it.

"Don't come back into that gym. All of you get cleaned up and move along to your next class. Do you understand?"

Juan hadn't moved. He was staying as still as possible, even though he was completely invisible. A few of the students began to trickle in as Shields watched them like an angry guard dog.

Juan couldn't believe what he was about to do, but he had to do it one last time. He cupped his hands over his mouth and screamed like a wounded animal. The sound reverberated off the walls, and everyone tore out of the locker room at breakneck speed. Shields stood flabbergasted, his eyes wide, revealing what Juan detected as fright. He screamed again, and this put it over the top. Shields stepped back and turned around, tucking tail, and running out into the gym.

Juan was laughing so hard he couldn't stop himself. Big, old, mean Mr. Shields afraid of ghosts. Juan was doubled over in hysterics. Then he heard the door squeak open again, and it was Shields peering around the corner, an aluminum bat in his hand.

Juan stared at him. His grin was so wide that his cheeks hurt. Shields glared back at him, the frightened look draining away from his face and being replaced by anger.

"What do you think you're doing?" he boomed.

Juan knew immediately that his Vest was gone. He was visible. "I . . . I . . ."

"Lurking in the locker room, shouting like that," Mr. Shields straightened up bravely.

"I wasn't lurking," Juan said, and in a way, it wasn't a lie. He had been out in the open; it's just that Mr. Shields hadn't been able to see him.

"Think that's funny, do you? What's your name?"

"Juan."

"Juan what?"

"Juan Ramirez."

"All right, Juan Ramirez," Shields barked, "you'll visit me during your lunch period, and you'll do some scrubbing."

"Scrubbing?" Juan raised his eyebrows.

"Scrubbing," Shields said, smiling wryly. "The rest of you can come in now. It was just a student."

Boys began trickling in reluctantly, staring at Juan before hurrying to change for their next class.

"See you at lunch, Mr. Ramirez," Shields said in a low

undertone.

"Yeah, okay," Juan said angrily.

"You address me as 'sir!'" Shields shouted with a sort of crazed grin.

"Okay, sir."

"Yes, sir!"

"Yes, sir," Juan said, a little louder.

Shields turned and walked out huffily. Juan couldn't help but think that Mr. Shields's angry disposition was all a front, especially after watching the big man bolt out of the locker room in utter terror when he had thought there was a ghost haunting the toilets.

"Scared me to death," said Josh, walking up to Juan and slapping him on the shoulder.

"Nice one," commented another boy.

"Yeah, nice one, Juan," Scottie Thomas said from across the room.

"Where were you?" Josh asked.

Juan smiled.

"Well, where were you hiding?"

"In a good spot," replied Juan.

"Yeah, I'll say. It sounded like you were right behind me in the stall."

"Maybe I was," Juan said, purposely sounding dark and mysterious.

"Uh . . . yeah," Josh stammered. "See ya later."

"See ya."

Chapter Six
Enter the Dark Vests

Three men stood together in the small open field bordered by large pine trees and wild huckleberry bushes that had been picked clean by black bears. The field was on a plateau overlooking the Wentachee River Canyon. Far below, the waters rushed through a maze of granite rock until finally reaching a large bend and flowing out of sight.

The plateau was isolated. No roads led up to it, and no houses were visible for miles around. A soft wind blew from the north, providing the men with some relief from the blazing sun.

The tallest of the three stood staring at the river below, his black eyes fixed on the water. He was a seven-foot tall, four hundred-pound Goliath — a giant compared to the others. He had thin dark black hair that hung past his almost pointed ears. He needed a shave, and large black hairs stuck out a half-inch from both his nostrils.

He took his eyes off the river and checked his watch, which barely fit around his massive wrist.

"Noon," he said gruffly. "Where is she?"

The person to his left was a brown-haired, brown-skinned man with a thin mustache and long sideburns that dove toward his jaw. His eyes were narrow, almost like slits, and his voice was high and raspy.

"She said she would be here quarter past eleven."

"Late as usual," the giant man said. "Old hag. We need a new Relocator. She's too old."

The third man was the shortest. His frame was bundled together with layers of fat that protruded most noticeably at his neckline and along his waistline and buttocks. He was bald, badly shaven, and spoke with a quiet subdued voice. "Yes, well that's not going to happen anytime soon, is it," he said plainly. "Not unless we get Jazmin, and that's not likely."

The giant grunted.

Suddenly, a shimmering flash of light appeared to the men's left, as if it had been dropped from the sky. The light grew brighter and began to take the shape of a large oval. Within the oval, a black liquid, like thick maple syrup, ran down from the top in a sort of waterfall. The black light grew more intense until the shape became very recognizable. It was a portal and through it walked the woman the giant man had called a hag.

She walked quickly, passing through the black goo waterfall without getting so much as a drop of it on her. She was a short, portly woman with long silver hair that flowed down to her waist. Her face was a maze of wrinkles, and her nose was pointed, almost like a needle. She wore a turtleneck sweater that was two sizes too big, and ripped and tattered pants. Her shoes had barely any soles left; most of her toes stuck out the front.

"About time, Thry," the giant said.

"Shut up, Strength," the old woman snarled. "Had a delay with a Laxintoth. Lucky I got here at all."

"It's always something with you," Strength said roughly. "I get sick of you always being late."

"Oh," Thry said with a cynical smile, "well, there are other alternatives like . . . walking. You'd best to watch it with me, Strength. I only tolerate you because I have to."

"Don't think I relish the thought of being near you, you stinking old maid. You're a disgrace to our kind."

"Yes, well, our kind needs me, don't they," she cackled. "Smelly or not, you need me."

Strength, who was nearly a foot and a half taller, walked up to the woman. "You'd better watch your tongue with me, woman. I could . . ."

"Could what?" came a deep voice from inside the black portal that still glimmered next to them.

Strength stepped back and watched as the man named Melt stepped through. He was dressed in all black and wore a dark hooded robe that swept down to his black boots. He wasn't as tall or as wide as Strength, but he was close. As he stepped up, Strength backed away.

"Could what?" Melt sneered.

"Yeah, could what?" the old woman echoed sharply.

"Nothing," Strength said in a whisper.

Melt looked at the three men. He knew all of them well. He had known Strength for almost five years, and although he had an incredible power, he was mentally weak. The man to Strength's left was Speed; named after the power given to him by a Chest. Speed was a follower, a sidekick and for now, he followed Strength. The fat, bald man was Imagination. Melt loathed him. Even though he had an enviable power, Melt couldn't stand lazy people.

Melt looked at Strength. "I am to give a report to Xylo this evening. He wants to know the progress on the new Brilliants."

Strength nodded submissively. "We traced them and have located all three now, sir."

"Well?"

Strength looked to Speed, who straightened up. "Two boys and a girl. They attend the same school and are all about the same age. I've seen each of their houses and know where to find them, sir."

"Have they been visited yet?"

"As far as we can tell . . . no," Speed answered.

"You are to wait then." Melt cracked a knuckle on his index finger. "You are to learn where they are meeting their Envoys. You know what you're to do after that."

"Sir," Strength spoke as evenly as possible, "how did Malavax do against the Laxintoth?"

Melt's lips curled into a small smile. "Like her, do you?"

"I asked because of its importance, sir, not because I like her."

"Of course, you did," Melt said, sarcastically. "She defeated it, and now we have three."

"Three, sir?" Speed asked, unbelievably.

"Three. Only four more and we have them all." Melt looked above them, toward the surrounding mountains.

"And what about the Liqwall? Did Ashton get the others?"

"No. He only got one. That puts our count at forty."

"Not bad, really," Imagination said proudly.

"No thanks to you," Melt spat. "You haven't captured one since you've been with us, Imagination. Now why is that? Your power is one of the best we have."

"I haven't had the right opportunity, sir," Imagination stammered.

"Please. You're an idiot, Imagination, letting yourself go like you have. I dislike you. You're not a worker like the other Shadows." Melt stepped forward, his face reddening. "You're lucky Xylo still approves of you because if it wasn't for him I would've melted you a long time ago."

Imagination's eyes widened with fear; his face turned ashen. "Yes . . . sir . . . "

Melt turned and looked at Thry, who wore an approving smile. "Take us back to the Triangle," he ordered.

Thry turned around and walked into the black portal with Melt right behind her. "Do your jobs," he said before walking under the waterfall of black syrup and vanishing.

The black portal exploded in a flash of black light and was gone.

"I hate him," Imagination shouted, shaking his fist.

"Just him?" Speed said angrily. "They're both so pompous. Think they're so important to the Shadows."

"They are," Strength said lowly. "I hate them, too;

Melt more than anything, but they're powerful Shadows. Never forget that, both of you. At least you're not assigned on a mission with them. Could you imagine?"

"No," Imagination said scornfully.

★ ★ ★

Juan hadn't wondered where Samantha and George were at lunch because he had been too busy scrubbing down the boys' locker room. Oh, if only he had remained invisible for just a little longer; then Mr. Shields wouldn't have been able to catch him. He wouldn't be scrubbing toilets and rinsing out sinks — not the most enjoyable things to do for thirty-five minutes when he should have been eating lunch.

Juan considered himself fortunate though. No one had seen him turn invisible, and he had Mrs. Rossin to thank for that. If she had followed her regular schedule of exercises and stretches, someone would have seen him disappear for sure. As much as he hated to admit it, Mrs. Rossin had unknowingly saved him this time.

But what about the next time he turned invisible? What would happen if he suddenly just disappeared during science lab? Juan could just see his lab partner, Jennifer Huron. She had to be one of the most paranoid people he'd ever met. If she saw him evaporate into nothing, they'd have to commit her.

Juan was growing less and less fond of his newfound power. Initially, the thought of going invisible sounded intriguing and exciting. But the more he thought about it, the more dangerous it seemed, and he realized he had a real potential to get into trouble or at least into a situation where he would have to answer questions he wanted to avoid.

Juan managed to finish the locker room to the satisfaction of Mr. Shields and had just enough time to slam down lunch before his afternoon classes, which he made it through still very much visible. At three o'clock he stood outside on the long, concrete sidewalk where lines of students waited for the buses. Juan rode the first one, driven by Mr. Fletcher. Since none of the buses left until three-fifteen, he had time to find Samantha and George.

He waited in the usual spot near the middle bench, excited to tell them what had happened during PE. Five minutes passed. Then ten. Students were beginning to file onto the buses, but Juan saw no sign of his friends. He waited a little longer, glancing often at his watch. Only two more minutes before the buses left. He surveyed the sidewalk one last time . . . nothing.

He sighed, turned, and headed toward the open doors

of the first bus. Just as he was about to step on, Samantha touched him on the shoulder.

"Where have you been?" he demanded, looking first at Samantha and then at George who stood behind her.

"It's a long story," she replied.

George leaned forward so that nosy old Mr. Fletcher couldn't hear. "Be at your window tonight at eleven, fully dressed. We need to talk."

Juan didn't question him. "Okay."

"Let's go, Juan," Mr. Fletcher called.

"I'll be waiting for you outside your window," George whispered before Juan started up the steps.

George turned to Samantha. "I'll pick you up a few minutes after eleven."

"What if you can't get your Vest?" Samantha asked, ready to get on her bus.

"If I'm not there by eleven-thirty, just figure I couldn't get it."

"Okay," she said, walking up the four steps and looking around the crowded bus. She saw a seat near the back and walked to it just as the bus started forward.

She slumped down on the green, lightly-cushioned bench seat next to Mickey Scrafford, a small spiky-haired sixth-grader who was very shy. His cheeks were the color of

Samantha's red backpack.

"Hi," she greeted pleasantly.

"H . . . h . . ."

Samantha turned. "Are you okay?"

"Fa . . . fa . . . fine," he stammered.

"Hey, Banks," called a voice two seats behind her. It was the unmistakable squawk of Paul Hertzinger. "Got yourself a boyfriend?"

She could hear his seventh and eighth-grade buddies laughing with him mockingly. "Scrafford, you're just a player," Paul teased.

It didn't seem possible, but Mickey turned an even darker shade of red.

Samantha, however, had not been embarrassed by the taunt. She turned back and glared menacingly at Paul. "Shut up!"

Paul puckered his lips and winked. "I know you want to go to the dance with me," he said smoothly.

"I'd rather you go in a lake and wipe your butt with the bubbles," Samantha said sharply, turning around.

The kids in the seats around her roared with laughter. Even Mickey cracked a smile through his red, puffy cheeks. That seemed to stop Paul, at least until Samantha stood up to move down the aisle as her stop approached.

That's when she felt something large and wet hit the back of her head. She turned and looked down. Next to her feet lay a chewed up, saliva-covered spitball, about half the size of a golf ball.

"Have a good day," Paul sneered.

Samantha ignored him as she made her way off the bus. As it pulled away from the curb, she could hear Paul shouting in a sing-songy voice from the open window. "Samantha, you know you want to go with me. Samantha's in love with me. Samantha's in love with Paully!"

As much as she wanted to turn and shout something that would have made her mother gasp, she didn't. Instead, she held her head high and walked down the street toward her house.

* * *

At a quarter to eleven that evening, George was standing in front of his open bedroom window. The night was fairly warm for September, and he had decided on jeans, a light sweater, and a windbreaker. He turned to look into the rectangular mirror above his bed on the opposite side of the room. Even though he wore a sweater and a coat, the Vest glimmered brightly, illuminating the room with golden light.

Getting his Vest had been easy. All he had needed to do was think about wanting it, to think about the power of flight, and it came. He hadn't been sure how easy it was going to be and around ten o'clock had started to practice acquiring it in the privacy of his bedroom just in case there was a problem. Once the Vest appeared, he would think about something else, and within a few moments, the lights softened and drained away until the outline of the Vest vanished. He would wait a few minutes and then concentrate on his power of flight, and again, the Vest appeared, just as bright and luminescent as it had been before.

He turned back toward the window, climbed onto the sill and jumped into the air, soaring high into the night sky like a bat. The light from the moon was glowing white, giving him more than enough light with which to see. Within a minute, he was soaring over the treetops and was high above the road, following it toward Juan's house.

As he flew in what he liked to think of as his Superman position, George wondered how fast he could really go. The wind was pushing against his face, causing his eyes to water and making him squint. He wasn't sure how fast he was going because he had nothing to gauge his speed with except his own perception. He began to think about flying faster, and just as quickly as he thought it, his speed picked up

— he was blazing through the night air, his jacket flapping wildly from the force of the wind.

'Way too fast,' he thought, slowing down to a more comfortable speed. The night was quiet and still, and as he saw Juan's house in the distance, he couldn't help but think what an incredible gift it was to be able to fly effortlessly. He understood clearly what the Chest meant when it said, "To you, the Gift . . ." because the ability to fly truly was a gift.

He circled Juan's house twice, looking for any signs that anyone might still be up, but the house was dark except for a light left on in the living room. George descended to the roof, paused to listen again, and then hovered outside Juan's window.

Juan was dressed in all black: pants, shirt, and a heavy coat. He was staring through the open window as George came into view. George hovered in front of it, still in his Superman position, as Juan climbed out and straddled his back.

"You all right?" George whispered.

"Yeah," Juan said quickly. "Go. Get out of here."

Juan gripped his coat as George rose into the air.

"What's going on?" Juan asked, a hint of apprehension in his voice. "Where are we going?"

"Got to pick up, Manthers," George said loudly, as Juan's house faded from view.

"Why?" Juan said, still whispering.

"You don't have to whisper," George reminded him. "I can barely hear you. We need to get her so we can tell you what happened today."

"Why? What happened?"

"Wait until I pick Samantha up," George said, veering left to avoid a very tall pine tree.

"Something happened to me today, too," Juan said, his apprehension now replaced by excitement.

"Really?" George turned his neck, looking at Juan through the corner of his eye.

"Yeah, it was during PE," Juan started, but George gave a sudden lurch to the right, and Juan stopped, grabbing George's coat collar a little tighter.

"Sorry about that," George said casually. "Almost hit an owl."

George's sudden movement made Juan realize the seriousness of what he was doing. Just a few days ago his life had been, for the most part, normal — and then one event, one strange and incredible event, had radically changed everything. And his life, along with those of his two best friends, was anything but normal now.

Juan decided to wait until they picked up Samantha to tell his story about PE and the locker room. He remained quiet and felt the wind push gently against his face as he watched trees, houses, driveways, and parked cars pass below. The city lights were closer and brighter now, and Juan could feel George ascending higher into the air, knowing that he was doing this because of the increased light from the streetlights and buildings.

Within a few minutes, George was hovering above Samantha's house. The neighborhood was quiet, and just as he had at Juan's house, he waited and surveyed everything before descending to the back of the house where Samantha's room was.

As he drew closer, he could make out the silhouette of Samantha's body in front of an open window. She was dressed warmer than Juan with a white parka, ski pants, and white gloves.

"For someone who's got the Vest of Knowledge, you don't dress well for sneaking out," George said, hovering next to the windowsill, allowing Samantha to climb on behind Juan.

"You don't wear white." Juan shook his head. "The object is not to be seen."

"Oh, shut up, both of you," Samantha barked in a whisper.

"You all set?" George asked.

"Ready," she said, putting her arms around Juan.

"Okay, here we go."

"We're lucky," Samantha said as George sped away, "that we all have our own rooms — would've been tough sneaking out if we didn't."

"Yeah," Juan agreed.

"You going to the Point?" Samantha asked George.

"Yep," he replied, heading toward a large plateau on the very western edge of the city.

The lights from the street lamps were fading. George used the bright moonlight once again to guide him higher, away from civilization. He glided over large trees and continued ascending for another five minutes before leveling out and circling a barren cliff that overlooked the city.

The Point, as Samantha had called it, was just that . . . an outcropping that overlooked Wenatchee, accessible only by four-wheel drive and only during daylight. No one was stupid enough, at least in Samantha's opinion, to try and drive out to it at night. The dirt road that led to it was littered with boulders, dips, ruts, and debris that could wreak havoc on any vehicle.

George landed softly on the ground, allowing Samantha and Juan to get off. Once they had, he stood up and stretched his arms toward the sky, his Vest shining brilliantly.

     "Well," Juan looked at both of them with anticipation, "what happened today?"

Chapter Seven

The Point

"Go ahead," George said, sitting down cross-legged on the rocky ground. "You tell him. You're the one who started it."

"Oh, right," said Samantha with an annoyed nod of her head. "I'm not the one that stood up in the middle of class and started shouting, 'Fire' like an imbecile."

"What are you two talking about?" Juan asked, frowning.

"We were in math with Mr. Dorn when I got my Vest. Just like that," Samantha said, snapping her fingers, "I knew everything about the lesson he was teaching. He was going on and on about negative numbers, and I knew everything about negative numbers."

"Then tell him what you did," George said sarcastically, rolling his eyes.

"I started to argue with him, and he got really mad," Samantha said matter-of-factly.

"Come on, Manthers. You didn't just argue with him."

"Why, what'd she do?" Juan was intrigued now.

"She stood up in the middle of class and shouted out the answers, claiming that she already knew everything there is to know about negative numbers. Old Dorn got frustrated and turned to the back of the book looking for some harder problems. He wrote some stuff I'd never seen on the board, and before he'd even finished, Samantha said the answer. It was crazy."

Samantha jumped in. "But then George stands up and says there's a fire in his shoe."

Juan started laughing. "A fire in your what?"

"Shoe," Samantha giggled.

"I was trying to distract them," George said defensively.

"By shouting that there was a fire in your shoe?" asked Juan in amazement.

"Hey, I had to think of something."

"Did it work?"

"No! Mr. Dorn sent us both to the office," Samantha responded with a shake of her head.

"And it didn't help when you shouted at him and slammed the door as we left either," George snapped.

"I didn't shout."

"Uh-huh."

"So what'd the principal do?" Juan asked.

"Well, we didn't get there right away because we ran into Paul . . . and he tried to kiss Samantha," George said flatly.

"What?" Juan asked, finally sitting down.

"Yeah, he did. He asked me to the dance and then leaned forward to try and kiss me. That's when George pushed him back, and they got in a fight."

"You got in a fight with Paul? Did ya win?"

"Nobody really won, because Mr. Spencer came out of his classroom and broke it up, but by then, we'd made too much noise and Dorn came out of his classroom madder than ever and walked us down to the office," George said, disgruntled.

"You guys are serious? This all happened today?"

"Yep, and all before lunch," Samantha said, sitting down beside her two friends.

"So what'd your parents say?" Juan asked, glancing back and forth at both of them as the light from George's Vest cast shadows across their faces.

"Our parents? They weren't as bad as the principal. You should've seen Mr. Lampert. He gave us all three days in-house." A look of anguish crossed George's face.

"Detention?"

"Yeah. I have to sit in a room all by myself and do homework. It's the most boring thing I've ever done," George said, rolling his eyes dramatically.

Samantha nodded in sympathy

"What about Paul? He got off?"

"Oh, no. He got in-house, too."

"You guys," Juan said, shaking his head disapprovingly.

There was a brief silence as the wind blew lightly over their faces, each of them looking at Wenatchee's glistening lights in the distance.

"Well, I went invisible today," Juan began, and he proceeded to tell Samantha and George everything from the time he turned invisible to the part where Mr. Shields saw him, and his wretched punishment.

"He made you clean the locker room during lunch?" George couldn't believe it.

"Yes," Juan said, clearly annoyed.

"That's got to be illegal or something," Samantha grumbled, waving her hand. "Teachers can't do that."

"Well, Shields did."

"Oh, I'm gettin' a headache," George said exhaustedly, rubbing his fingers along his temples. "I'm really tired."

Samantha glanced down at her watch. "It's twelve-thirty."

"So what are we going to do?" asked George, the light from his Vest still brightly illuminating everything around them.

"Juan, have you figured out how to get your Vest on and off?" Samantha wondered. "George and I were discussing it after school before we saw you. It's simple really."

And in a moment her Vest appeared over her white parka.

"Aren't you hot with that coat on? It's not that cold out."

"It's perfect. Now listen," Samantha stated, getting back to the subject. "To get your Vest, you must concentrate on the power."

"Yeah, I figured as much."

"And to get it off, you must think it off or just concentrate on something else."

"I had a little trouble with that earlier in the locker room. I tried to think it off, but it wouldn't go away. I think I'm beginning to get the hang of it now though," Juan said, just before turning completely invisible.

"Whoa!" Samantha leaned back in surprise. "You changed quick. I can't see you at all."

"Or my Vest?"

"Nothing. I can't see any part of you or the Vest. That's

weird. . . ."

"What do you mean?" asked Juan.

"I can see George's Vest when he has it on, and I can see mine when I have mine on, but I can't see yours. It must be part of the Gift. Even though you have your Vest, no one can see it."

"My head," George mumbled softly, running his hand through his long hair that for once wasn't tied in a ponytail.

"George, it's your Vest that's causing you to feel that way."

"What?"

"Yes, yes," Samantha said almost to herself, the thoughts plopping into her mind like sugar cubes into coffee. "You're getting fatigued."

"Fa . . . what?" George mumbled.

"Fatigued," she repeated patiently. "You're getting tired because you've had your Vest on for a long time. When you do, you get tired. That's what's causing your headache and why you feel so exhausted. Take the Vest off."

George shut his eyes and in a couple of seconds, his Vest faded away, along with the headache.

"Amazing," he breathed deeply, standing up and stretching.

"You're going to need to rest awhile before you fly us

home," Samantha noted, her own Vest glimmering. "It takes some time for the effects to wear off."

Juan suddenly reappeared, standing and grinning with pleasure.

"I tried doing this in the locker room, and now, it's like . . . no problem," he said happily, thinking that he at last had control over his power.

As Samantha stood up to brush herself off, she noticed a light beginning to emerge off to her right as though it were piercing the air itself, and it wasn't coming from her glowing Vest. Instead, this light swirled around in circles, growing larger with each revolution.

"What is it?" Juan whispered.

"I don't know," Samantha said, watching as the glowing light took shape in the form of what looked like a picture frame, glittering with the same color and brilliance as Samantha's Vest.

From within the frame, a darker yellow light pulsated brightly until the inside was filled with it. Then an image began to come into focus. Samantha knew immediately what is was. She had seen it many times before. It was the old, decaying barn at the fairgrounds.

"The barn," she whispered, watching intently as the picture cleared. It was as though they were watching a glowing television screen. "That's the barn at the fairgrounds."

"What?" Juan asked, bewildered.

"Yeah, you're right," said George, recognizing the structure. "Why is there a picture of that old thing?"

"YOU ARE TO MEET HERE AT THE BARN ON SAT-URDAY, SEPTEMBER TWENTY-FIFTH, AT NOON," said the same voice they had heard that day in Boulder Cave when they had received their powers. "THERE YOU WILL MEET THREE VESTS — YOUR ENVOYS — AND BE GIVEN FURTHER IN-STRUCTIONS."

Just like the Chest had done in the cave, the frame exploded in a blinding flash of white light and was gone.

"What the . . ." Juan managed to utter.

"What was it, Samantha?" George looked at her seriously. "Come on, your Vest has to be telling you."

But he could tell by the expression on her face that she didn't know. "I'm not getting anything," she whispered, disappointed.

"Okay . . . so . . . September twenty-fifth . . . noon . . . at the old barn at the fair," Juan echoed, not entirely sure he had heard the voice correctly.

"That's what I heard," George added.

"What did it mean by 'instructions?'"

"I don't know, Manthers. Maybe we're going to get

some kind of special instructions or something," George guessed.

"Well, yeah, I figured that, but what kind of instructions?"

"This is gettin' weird," muttered Juan, looking worried. "First the Chest in the cave and now this. We should've never opened that thing."

"We? I was the one that opened it," George said, dismayed. "You and Samantha told me not to, but I just had to see what was inside."

"September twenty-fifth isn't that far off," Samantha said pensively. "We're going to have to make sure we're all at the fairgrounds by noon."

"Right." Juan nodded. "But in the meantime, I've got to watch it with my Vest. I can't be turning invisible in PE anymore. I got lucky, but I can't let that happen again."

"We all have to watch it," George ordered, glaring at Samantha. "We need to agree not to use our powers in school when others are around. Agreed?"

"Yeah."

"Okay," Samantha concurred.

George lay down on the ground, and instantly his Vest exploded into light around him. "Get on. It's time to go home."

"How's your head?" Samantha asked, climbing onto his back first.

"Hurts," he said. "But not as bad. Come on Juan, let's go."

Juan sat behind Samantha and held on to her waist as George ascended into the sky, leaving the Point and soaring high overheard toward Samantha's house. Even if they had looked back, they wouldn't have been able to see the men emerge from the rock wall, slightly above where they had just been. Each wore black clothing from head to toe, including black Vests.

"Couldn't have asked for anything better," Strength said, stepping closer to the edge and looking at the silhouettes flying away in the distance.

"September twenty-fifth. Noon at a fairground," Speed spoke slowly.

"Right," Strength said in a low tone. "Must be the local fair."

Imagination turned and faced the rock wall from which he, Strength, and Speed had emerged. He raised his arm and the rock began to dissolve until it faded away into nothing.

"Nice rock, Imag," Strength said, pointing to where it had just been. "I wasn't sure they would actually go through with it, sneaking out in the middle of the night. These three got guts."

"I didn't think they'd do it either. And with the Will showing itself like it did, it's perfect. Everything is working out better than we planned. So, do we go forward with stage one?" Imagination looked at Strength's shadowy face, which was partially illuminated by the moonlight.

"Yes. I'll signal Thry and you create them now. By the time we return, they'll have taken care of the girl. We'll wait to see if Melt's plans have changed for the two boys."

Imagination nodded and closed his eyes. As he raised his arms, a sparkling black light flickered from the end of each of his fingers. Two creatures appeared, wings extended and flapping above him.

"Come down," he ordered and the mammoth creations obeyed, landing and retracting their wings.

Even Strength, who had served with Imagination for years, was amazed at what stood before him. They were like a cross between some species of dinosaur and a bird. Each creature looked identical, and as Strength admired them, he thought they closely resembled a tyrannosaurus rex, albeit, a smaller version. Both creations were eight-feet tall and stood on two powerful legs. Instead of feet, there were five razor-sharp, glistening black claws. Their torsos were thick, and two long arms equipped with sharp talons protruded from the sides of their bodies. They had long necks with the exact shape and dimension of the extinct scavenger. Their bodies were a scaly mixture of green and brown, and their wings were folded tightly in against their backs. Their eyes were large and the pupils were vertical, like a cat's. The more Strength scanned them, the more impressed he became. These were frightening creations. Imagination had done well.

"You know what you must do," Imagination spoke to the winged dinosaurs. "Destroy the girl."

Both creatures opened their mouths, exposing their jaws lined with gigantic, sharply pointed teeth. They let out a hideous round of sounds, waiting for Imagination to give the final order.

He pointed in the direction Samantha, George, and Juan had taken and said, "Go."

The creatures spread their wings, let out another barrage of shrill cries, and lifted into the air, flapping with such power they sounded like helicopters taking off. Strength, Speed, and Imagination watched as they followed the path George had flown.

"Impressive," Strength marveled, stepping forward and looking down at his watch. He pushed the only button on it, and in a moment the screen turned white and glowed. He waited until he saw the face he sought.

"Fingust," he said, bringing the watch closer to his face.

"What is it?" the old man in the watch screen asked.

"We need Thry. Tell her we're ready for pick up. You have our coordinates?"

The old man looked down at something and then back up. "Yes," he said coldly. "I will tell her."

Strength pushed the watch button again and the old man faded away, along with the glow.

"This should be an interesting couple of days," Strength hissed wickedly. "It's time for the three Vests to meet the power of the Shadows."

Chapter Eight
The Dream

By the time Samantha had finally changed into her pajamas, she could barely keep her eyes open. When her head hit the pillow, she was sound asleep and it wasn't long before she was immersed in a recurring dream she'd been having the last two nights.

She was at the Y, a popular river beach ten miles out of town, talking with her friends, and at the same time, eyeing Greg Jackson, one of the most popular and good-looking boys in seventh grade. Staring over at him, she felt herself go warm all over when his eyes met hers.

She had to be bold, she had to be the one to make the first move she told herself because Greg was inherently shy and hardly ever said a word to her. She took a few steps toward him, their eyes still locked together. What was she going to say? Her heart was racing. She was getting closer. And just as she was opening her mouth to speak, an old, gray-bearded man came out of nowhere and stepped in front of her.

"Move along, you people," the old man said, shooing the group of five boys away. Greg looked at Samantha disappointedly before turning to leave with the others.

"Who are you?" Samantha asked, clearly agitated.

The old man was tall and looked down at her through thick spectacles while stroking his mangy beard. Samantha eyed him from head to toe. He was wearing black boots, big blue overalls, and a flannel shirt.

"Nathaniel," he said warmly.

"Well, you just . . ." Samantha leaned and looked over at Greg who was now talking with his group of friends. "Never mind," she said, walking around the old man.

"We don't have time for that," Nathaniel spoke quickly. "Really. We don't."

"What are you talking about?" Samantha turned. "We have plenty of time."

"No, we don't," the strange man said, waving his hands. In an instant, Greg, along with his pack of friends, disappeared.

"Where'd he go?" Samantha shouted.

"Away." Nathaniel smiled and a bright light circled out of his hands, forcing Samantha to shut her eyes. But how could she be shutting her eyes? She was dreaming. Her eyes were already shut.

When she finally opened them, she was no longer on the beach. She was in a room and everywhere she looked were musical instruments — glowing musical instruments of every kind floated magically in the air. There was a trumpet, a flute, a violin . . . each hovering above glowing white chairs. Larger instruments like the cello, the double bass, and the tuba floated alongside their respective chairs.

"Quite amazing, don't you think?" Nathaniel asked, a smile of pure joy on his face. "Welcome to the Music Room. If you'll follow me please —" He motioned to Samantha with his hand.

She followed him, soon realizing she wasn't walking, but rather gliding smoothly in the air a few inches from the glowing white floor. Nathaniel led her down one of the small aisles, past many stringed instruments, some of which she had never seen before, until finally stopping directly in the center of the room.

Glowing balls of light the size of bowling balls hovered from the ceiling high above, but as Samantha looked more carefully, she realized there were no electrical cords nor were they hung by any sort of wire or string. They were simply floating.

"Wonderful, isn't it?" the old man cackled happily. "Like this place, do you?"

"Uh, yeah," Samantha uttered.

"Might very well visit here some day, although the

chance of you actually hearing something is very unlikely."

Samantha had no idea what Nathaniel was talking about.

"Well, this is it," he said, putting his hand on the magnificent looking grand piano that shimmered in golden light. "Now I want you to listen carefully. . . ."

He sat down on the elaborately carved wooden bench, cracked his fingers as though he was about to give a recital, and then placed his index finger down and pushed one of the white keys.

A note rang out, echoing loudly, and then faded away. Nathaniel looked up at Samantha hopefully. "Well?"

"Well, what?"

"What did you hear?"

"A . . . a musical note."

"Really?"

Nathaniel returned his attention to the keys, placed both hands down and played a long full chord. At first Samantha heard music but suddenly, the music turned into words, into the words . . .

Hello, Samantha.

Samantha looked around nervously. Was she supposed to hear that?

Nathaniel looked up again. "Hear anything that

time?"

Samantha hesitated. She didn't know what to say.

"Well?"

"I . . . heard . . . words. . . ."

Nathaniel leapt to his feet. "Really! You heard words? What did she say?"

"Who?" Samantha looked around.

"Cfage. What did Cfage say?"

"Who's Cfage?"

Nathaniel smiled happily. "The piano."

"Ah," Samantha mumbled. "It, I mean she . . . well, she said . . . said . . . 'hello, Samantha.'"

Nathaniel clapped his hands together. "Wonderful. This is fantastic. So it's you!"

"Me?" Samantha was completely confused.

"Let's try again." Nathaniel returned to the bench and struck two more quick chords.

SAMANTHA, YOU ARE IN . . .

"It said that I was in . . ." Samantha said, shrugging.

"In what?"

"Didn't say."

Nathaniel played another chord.

. . . DANGER.

"Danger," Samantha said hastily.

Nathaniel turned his head, his face extremely serious. Then he played a series of notes and chords.

You are being hunted by Imagination. Open your right hand and close your eyes. When you feel it inside your hand, clasp your fingers around it.

Nathaniel kept playing.

It will help you to defend yourself. Now, close your eyes.

Samantha closed her eyes, opened her right hand and felt something round and soft placed in her palm.

Nathaniel pounded the keys vigorously.

Here they come. Open your eyes now!

Samantha opened her eyes. She was in her bed, staring up at the dark ceiling. She propped herself up, and then looked at her right hand that was clenched over something. She opened her fingers and saw a glowing ball pulsating brilliantly in her palm. What was it? What was it supposed to do? And hadn't that been a dream? Who was Nathaniel? Where had she been?

The shattering glass made her scream as the first of Imagination's creatures lunged forward through the broken window, snapping its jaws wildly at her. She rolled off the bed and flung the bedroom door open, screaming in terror. Her legs were like rubber. She could hear the whatever-theyweres behind her, shrieking in what sounded like high-pitched barks.

Then to her left, the bedroom door opened and there stood her youngest brother, Chris. "What's wrong?" he asked, wide-eyed.

"They're coming to get me!" Samantha shouted, running down the hall past him as fast as she could.

"What are you talking . . ."

But Chris didn't finish his sentence because he was suddenly and violently pushed backward by something he hadn't seen. He fell to the floor and hit his head against the base of the dresser.

Samantha stopped at the top of the stairs. The creatures were upon her now, only a few feet away. The bedroom door to her right suddenly opened, and her other two brothers, Brian and Jack, ran out.

"What is it?" Brian said, staring at a crazed Samantha.

"Look out!" Samantha screamed, but neither of her brothers saw the dinosaur as it had turned around, lowered its head, and charged into them. The impact sent them reeling back into their room.

Samantha was crying, running down the stairs as fast as she could. There were sounds coming from downstairs . . . voices . . . her parents.

"Dad!" Samantha shrieked, charging into the kitchen just as her dad flipped on the light.

"What's going on?"

"They're coming to get me," Samantha wailed.

"Who?" Her dad looked around feverishly.

"Those!" She pointed as the two creatures entered the kitchen, growling and hissing wickedly at her.

"What honey?"

"Right there, can't you see them?" Samantha shouted, pointing with a shaking finger.

"What?" Her dad looked baffled. "I don't see anything."

The creatures were inching closer.

"Samantha, what is going on?" Her mother came dashing into the kitchen in a nightgown.

The sudden movement frightened the creatures and the closest one lunged at Mrs. Banks so quickly that Samantha couldn't even warn her. The creature's jaws wrapped around Mrs. Banks's shoulder, picked her up, and tossed her over the kitchen table.

Mr. Banks whipped around, grabbing the largest butcher knife he could from the cutlery cube.

"Who's here!" he shouted.

"Dad . . . Dad!"

The creatures were now only a few steps away.

"I can't see them, honey. Where are they?"

"Right in front of . . ."

But before she could finish, one of the creatures used its long, scaly arm to knock the knife out of her father's unsuspecting hand. Before he had time to react, it drove its head into his chest. The blow knocked the wind out of him, and he fell to the floor, gasping for air.

The things inched closer — sniffing and growling loudly, examining her like she was a piece of meat about to be devoured.

"Hey, where are they?" she heard Brian yell, as he charged into the kitchen with an aluminum baseball bat.

"Right in front of me," Samantha screamed.

Brian swung the bat like a blind man back and forth, taking steps closer and closer. The creatures turned, but the second one didn't move in time, and the side of the bat collided with its head.

Brian went white with the realization that he'd just hit something that was invisible. He swung again and caught the dazed creature across the jaw. It fell to the floor with a hard thump.

The second dinosaur reacted and charged, ramming into Brain's body, propelling him backward until he slammed into the wall with a sickening thud. It turned its ugly head to look down at its twin, and that's when Samantha felt the ball of light in her hand shaking spasmodically. She opened her palm and stared at it as it pulsated brightly, vibrating so fast it was almost a blur.

Then she realized what she needed to do. "I need my Vest!" she shouted.

In an instant, the shape of a glowing white Vest covered her upper body. The creature turned its attention back to Samantha and let out a shriek so loud that she wanted to cup her hands over her ears, but she couldn't. She had only seconds to concentrate on the creature.

'What is it? How do I make it stop?' she asked herself.

The thought immediately came. IT'S NOT REAL. DON'T BELIEVE IN IT AND IT WON'T BE.

"You're not real!" Samantha yelled. "You're not real!"

The creature howled again and stepped forward, exposing its sharp teeth. She could feel and smell its hot, rancid breath.

THEY'RE ONLY IMAGINARY. THEY EXIST ONLY IF YOU BELIEVE THEY ARE REAL.

"You're not real, you don't exist!" Samantha shouted.

The creature lunged.

"You're not real! YOU'RE NOT REAL!"

In a fiery blast of light, both creatures disintegrated.

She stood, rooted to the spot, shaking with fear. Her father was getting to his feet, and finally managed to stand up.

"Are you all right?" he whispered. "Samantha?"

Samantha couldn't speak. She looked in her hand and stared at the glowing ball of light. It grew brighter and brighter until she could no longer look at it. She turned her head and closed her eyes.

"Are you all right?" she heard her father ask again.

Samantha opened her eyes to see her father sitting on the edge of the bed, looking down at her gently, and her mother standing beside him.

"Dad," she whispered hoarsely.

"You were having a nightmare."

"What?"

"You were having a bad dream, Sam. It's all right now. Everything's okay," her dad said comfortingly.

"But the dinosaurs . . ."

"No dinosaurs, honey. That was just your imagination. Go to sleep now, okay? Just sleep."

Her dad kissed her on the forehead and her mother gently touched her cheek. "Go back to sleep," she said and flipped off the light before shutting the door.

Samantha was sweating and shaking. She was still

petrified. She propped herself up on the bed and looked at her hands. The glowing ball was gone. Everything was gone. Everything but her fear. That hadn't been a nightmare. She'd had nightmares before. Something about that had been eerily real.

Chapter Nine
The Hooked Nose

George's bus was the last to arrive the next morning at Eagle Crest Middle School. When he stepped off, Samantha pulled so hard on his long-sleeved shirt that it ripped at the shoulder.

"What are you doing?" he gasped, as Samantha led him away from the bus.

"Hey, George," Juan called from a nearby bench.

Samantha looked around hastily and beckoned George to sit down next to Juan, but he was too busy examining his sleeve.

"Did you have it?" Samantha said quietly so that only George and Juan could hear as other students passed by.

"Have what?" George asked, still eyeing his ripped sleeve. "This was a new shirt, Manthers. You didn't have to pull me like that."

"Sorry," she said quickly. "But did you have it?"

"What are you talking about?"

"The dream. Did you have the dream?"

"What dream?"

"About the dinosaurs," Samantha said anxiously.

"No," replied George irritably.

"What about the girl?" Juan spoke in a rush.

George gave Samantha and Juan a bewildered look. "I don't know what you guys are talking about."

Samantha looked at Juan, who shrugged.

"Something happened last night. . . ."

And she proceeded to tell George everything. All the way up to her parents standing next to her bed and telling her it had all been a nightmare.

"I don't see what's so special about that, Manthers. I mean, yeah, you had a bad dream that seemed real. Haven't you ever had one like that before?"

"Not like that!"

"I had almost the exact same dream," Juan said quietly, "minus the dinosaurs and the glowing ball."

George raised his eyebrows. "What do you mean?"

"Last night I had a dream that I was playing soccer when a small girl came into the field and started ordering everyone away. It was like she was real or something. Then the scenery changed, and I ended up in the room Samantha told you about, the room with all the instruments. The girl led me over to the piano, to the same piano Samantha mentioned."

George was looking more serious as Juan continued. "The little girl started playing the piano and asking me what I heard, but I didn't hear . . ."

"Anything," George said flatly.

Juan's eyes flashed. "What?"

"The little girl pounded on the keys, but you didn't hear anything, right?"

"That's right!"

"You had the dream then?" Samantha asked, looking at George excitedly.

"I guess I did," George said slowly looking past her, his thoughts rewinding to last night. "When you started talking about it Juan, it just came back to me. I was in a room just like you, but there wasn't a little girl. It was a boy, and he kept asking me what I heard. I kept telling him I couldn't hear anything."

"Yeah, so did I," Juan said enthusiastically. "Did he seem . . . disappointed?"

"Uh huh. When he finally stopped playing, he stood up, and it looked like he was crying."

"Then what happened?" Samantha asked.

"Everything went away."

"Me, too," said Juan.

"But I didn't have anything like those dinosaur things you were talking about — that's creepy."

"It seemed so real," Samantha said, her voice shaking as she thought about her dream again. "This morning I got my Vest and tried to find out what it meant, but it didn't tell me anything."

"A few days ago our lives were normal, and now we can't even sleep without having funky dreams," George said, shaking his head.

The synthesized bell rang, which meant they only had a few more minutes to get to their first-period class. They hadn't noticed that, except for a few stray students being dropped off by their parents, they were the only ones still outside.

They made their way through the doors and inside to the busyness of student traffic.

"Let's talk more at lunch," Juan said, sliding out of the way of other incoming students.

"We can't. We still have in-house, remember?"

"Oh, yeah. Sorry. After school then."

"Right."

"Hey, remember," Samantha said quietly, "we don't use our Vests at school."

"Yes, I know," Juan said, glancing at his watch. "Let's

meet outside by the bench right after classes get out."

Juan and George strode off together toward their locker, while Samantha headed in the opposite direction to her own locker.

* * *

In-house detention was boring, even for Paul Hertzinger. No one got to do anything remotely fun. Each of them were in separate rooms, piled with menial schoolwork that had to be completed by the end of their detentions or they would have three more days of it.

Even if Samantha had used her Vest, it wouldn't have helped much. The work she was assigned resembled what she had done in third grade; the power of knowledge wouldn't help her copy short cursive sentences any faster. Sentences like: THE TREE IS GREEN. THE SHIP SAILED INTO THE SEA and others. And when something is boring, time creeps along, which explained why Samantha stared at the clock most of the time.

As she copied the sentences over and over, her mind replayed the events of the last few days — from the moment the light had hit her in the cave to the dream that had seemed so real. Even though she had mulled the events over many times, it wasn't helping. There were still so many questions and so few answers.

When three o'clock finally arrived, she shoved her books into her backpack, turned in her work to Mrs. Lassen, the principal's secretary, and waited for George. Together, they met up with Juan at the bench as hundreds of students stood around talking and waiting to get on their buses.

"That was so boring," Samantha said, slumping down on the bench.

"I fell asleep with my head on the table for about fifteen minutes," George admitted, sitting down next to her. "I wish they didn't put us in separate rooms. I was hoping we'd be together at least. Doing this stuff is worse than science class."

"You don't like science?" Samantha looked shocked.

"With Mrs. Treehouse? Are you kidding?"

"It's not Treehouse." Samantha frowned. "It's Treehaus."

"Whatever. She's just about as boring as sitting in there doing those ridiculous sentences," George said, gruffly.

"Well, I don't think so. She's been really fun this year."

"Fun? Listening to her lecture all the time is fun?"

"The lectures are very interesting," said Samantha defensively.

"Yeah, if you're dead."

"Excuse me — can we figure out what we're doing, 'cause the buses are getting ready to leave," said Juan nervously. "Should we meet tonight?"

"No!" Samantha and George snapped in unison.

"I can't risk it. My dad is still mad at me for getting detention."

"Mine too," Samantha agreed. "We'd better not tonight."

"Okay then," Juan said, starting toward his bus.

"Wait . . . Juan," Samantha got up and followed him. "Did you, you know, have any . . ."

"No," Juan said in a hushed voice, looking over his shoulder. "Everything was fine. Just didn't think about it."

"Good. Okay, well, I'll see you tomorrow."

"Yeah. See you, George."

"See you." George gave a short wave and made his way toward his bus.

As difficult as it had been, Juan had tried not to think about his power. He had attempted to concentrate on his lessons and assignments, hoping that by doing so, he would keep his mind off the power of invisibility. However, there had been a few moments during his most boring class, keyboarding with Mrs. Ulra, that he began thinking about how great it would be to go invisible and leave the class. Typing the home row letters repeatedly for thirty minutes was torture, especially since Juan already knew how to type thirty words per minute, and Mrs. Ulra insisted he be on the same page, doing the same lessons as the rest of the class. She drove him nuts.

The bus ride home was the usual bore, and Juan wondered just how old the bus really was. He didn't think he'd ever felt the yellow beast go more than forty miles an hour, and if it ever did, the seats would probably shudder violently in protest. The bus reached Juan's house, and when he got off, he sprinted down the gravel driveway to avoid the cloud of black smoke it belched as it pulled away.

Walking toward a small, red, two-door sedan was Juan's oldest sister, Angelica, her long, black hair pulled back in a ponytail which swayed from side to side as she walked.

Angelica was a senior in high school and ended her school day about noon. Between her job at the clothing store and her cross-county practices, Juan hardly ever saw her. She was smart, athletic, and one of the few people Juan trusted with important and secret information — like the time he blew out the sliding glass door with the BB gun — because he knew she would never tell anyone.

"Where ya goin'?" he asked.

"Down to Vanity's Look," she answered, opening the

car door.

"Can I come?"

"To Vanity's Look?" Angelica looked at him puzzled. "It's a women's . . ."

"I know what it is," Juan broke in. "Just drop me off at the Hooked Nose. It's only a couple blocks before."

"But I'm not going to be at Vanity long."

"Fine. Just drop me off and pick me up when you're done."

"Why? What do you need at the Hooked Nose?" Angelica asked him, climbing in the car. Juan went around to the other side and got in, throwing his pack in the back seat.

"I want to look at their new fishing rods."

"Oh, how exciting," Angelica said sarcastically.

"It's a lot more exciting than looking at pants," Juan shot back.

"I'm looking for a new blouse."

"Oh, even better."

It took Angelica a few tries before she got the car started. She backed out of the driveway and onto the highway that led to Wenatchee.

"How do you like middle school?" she asked, turning her head to look at Juan for a moment.

"It's okay. I don't like keyboarding though."

"Who do you have?"

"Mrs. Ulra."

"Too bad. She makes life so dull."

"That class goes by the slowest. What about you? How's senior year, since I never get to see you?"

"Busy. I don't have to go into work until five tonight, and Coach Hicks was sick, so I actually have an afternoon to do some stuff," Angelica said, pushing the volume button on the CD player so that her Latino music blared loudly. Juan didn't mind except when she played it so loud that the windows shook.

The Hooked Nose was a warehouse-sized store of nothing but sporting goods, named after the nose a spawning Chinook salmon develops after entering fresh water. If there was something you needed related to fishing or hunting, this store had it, or if they didn't, they could get it for you. It was by far Juan's favorite place to shop.

"Okay, I'll be back here in about an hour. Be outside," Angelica said as Juan scurried out of the car.

"Right. One hour," he said, slamming the door and heading into the store.

He jetted off to the right, toward the east wall and the fishing supplies. He made his way past displays of hunting vests, duck decoys, and camouflage coats, going directly to the massive assortment of fishing poles that lined the wall. Poles of all sizes, from thick to thin, tall to short, black to fluorescent yellow . . . there was every kind of pole imaginable.

It looked like the store had gotten a new shipment in because he didn't remember seeing this large of an assortment before. This would take more than an hour, he thought, surveying the collection. He would work his way down systematically, looking especially for a ten-foot, six-inch, medium-feel salmon rod. September was prime season for fall run Chinook salmon, and maybe the upcoming weekend would lend itself to some fishing.

Juan longed for a new pole. The one he used for catching large salmon wasn't long or strong enough. He had hooked a large fish last year that nearly broke his pole in half before the big fish shook the hook loose and got away.

He strolled along the aisle, occasionally stopping and picking up one of the poles, feeling its weight and sensitivity. He was holding a six-and-a-half-foot black trout rod when he heard someone yell so loud it echoed throughout the store. It was a shriek of fright, and when Juan heard it, the hairs on the back of his neck prickled up, and he felt a cold shiver pass through him.

There was another shriek. This one sounded like a woman . . . loud like the last one, but cut off suddenly, as though someone had put a hand over her mouth. Then Juan heard a sound he'd never heard before — like that of an animal, but what kind of animal he didn't know. He looked up and down the aisle in panic.

Another animal growl and a yell from someone else — this time Juan dropped the pole. His mind was telling him to run, to get out as fast as he could. As near as he could tell the screams were coming from the front of the store, and the only way in and out was through the front door.

A thought entered his mind, and he acted on it. Closing his eyes and concentrating hard, he thought about his Vest, about his power of invisibility. And when he opened his eyes a few moments later, his brilliant Vest had wrapped itself around him.

He was invisible.

He crept up the aisle, being careful to make as little noise as possible. Another scream from someone else sounded like it came from the next aisle over. Juan froze, his breath coming in short, swift gasps. He felt cold sweat on his forehead; his hands were like ice.

He waited.

Nothing.

The store was silent . . . silent like it had never been before.

Juan stood, listening hard.

Deathly quiet.

The blur ran past him so fast that the force of the wind nearly knocked him over. He turned to follow it with his eyes, but the black shadow had vanished. What had that been?

Juan remembered something George had said about seeing some sort of blur the night he had flown to the river. Had that been what he had just seen? He gulped, swallowing the build up of saliva in his mouth, and took five quiet but brave steps to the corner, looking around the end toward the front of the store.

The first thing to catch his eye was the man lying on the floor, face down, not moving. He must've been a customer because he wasn't wearing a red Hooked Nose shirt. Juan stared at the man, and felt a little relief when he saw that he was breathing, even though he was unconscious.

Juan looked toward the front checkout counter where two employees, a man and a woman wearing Hook Nose shirts were slumped over the counter, face down and unconscious. Juan's hands were shaking and what felt like a rock had just landed in his stomach. He had to get out of there. He had to get to the door.

He took another six steps toward the entrance. There wasn't any movement or sound. Juan had never imagined that his favorite store could be so hauntingly scary. He took another seven steps. He was closer. He could see the glass doors that led to safety. If he sprinted, he could get there in a few seconds. He leaned forward and was about ready to go into an all-out run when he saw a massive man step out from behind one of the displays of duck decoys, scanning the room menacingly.

"Speed," he called roughly. "Anything?"

Juan stood still, his mouth so wide he could've jammed a golf ball in it. Who was that man? Who was he talking to? And what was that thing around . . . his . . . chest? That's when Juan realized what he was staring at. Across the man's thick chest was a Vest of Dark Light, sparkling and glimmering just like his own, except that it was black.

A blur of dark light came speeding toward the man and stopped directly in front of him.

"Nothing," Speed reported.

"But we saw the boy come in here," Strength said gruffly.

The voice that came from behind Juan scared him so badly that his scream stuck in his throat. It was a good thing it had because the man standing next to him had no idea Juan was there.

"It is possible," Imagination said, looking above at the

lights and the rafters, "that the boy went invisible."

Juan turned his head slowly, and standing not two feet away from him was a third man with a Dark Vest.

"Seal the doors," Strength said.

Juan watched Imagination raise his hands and then heard a loud CATHUNK. He looked toward the entrance and saw that there were now giant black pieces of wall where the glass doors had once been.

"That will keep him from getting out without us knowing about it."

"We won't have much time with the doors like that," Speed said in his high-pitched voice.

"Yes, I know," Strength agreed. "Imagination, is there anything you can create to help us see the boy?"

"No," Imagination said, "but I could create a gas that will knock him out, and when he becomes unconscious, he'll be visible."

"What about us?" Speed asked.

"I'll give us each masks."

"Do it," Strength ordered.

Juan didn't know who these men were, but he had sense enough to know that they were evil — they knew about him and about his power of invisibility. And there was now a man standing close to him who apparently had the ability to make anything he thought of. Three masks appeared over the men's faces at exactly the same time, and not a second later, a white gas began to surround Juan's feet, as though it was being released from vents in the floor.

He turned and, forgetting about stealth, sprinted down the fishing pole aisle until he made his way to the back wall. He could hear muffled voices speaking through the masks.

The gas was becoming denser. Juan was getting light-headed, and he could feel his chest tightening. He didn't know exactly how long he had left before the gas knocked him out, but he figured it wouldn't be long before he slipped into unconsciousness.

He hurried along the back wall, holding his breath in intervals and looking for an exit or someplace to hide. But the gas was everywhere. He turned and could barely make out the two gray, swinging doors that led to the back of the store where surplus inventory was kept. He ran through, blasting the doors open, and looked around frantically. He knew the men must've heard the doors, but he didn't care.

He took a few steps to his left, and there was his escape. Two large yellow doors, twelve-feet tall, were all that stood between him and breathable air. His lungs were burning, his eyes watering, and everything was spinning, but he had to concentrate. He ran to the doors and looked for a knob. There was none. He looked to the right, searching for anything that might unlock them. Then he saw it — a large red button on the wall.

He heard the doors swing open behind him. The men were close. Juan pushed the red button and heard a loud click, before they swung outward automatically and bright sunlight, coupled with fresh air came pouring in. He ran as hard as he could out into the open and away from the store before finally collapsing next to a locust tree.

He was shaking almost uncontrollably and closed his eyes, trying to calm down. His chest was loosening up and when he finally opened his eyes again, the surrounding landscape had stopped spinning, and he could finally breathe normally. But when Juan saw the three men in masks step out into the sunlight, he gasped and held his breath again. He looked down at his shirt, relieved to see that his Vest was still aglow.

Strength ripped off his mask and looked around angrily. He swore repeatedly as Imagination and Speed removed their masks.

"We had him," Imagination said, looking around feverishly. "Never even thought about the back loading doors."

"Neither did I," Strength grunted. "Xylo will not be

pleased when he finds out that another one got away."

"I could create a cage of . . ."

Strength cut off Imagination's suggestion. "It won't do any good. We've already brought enough attention to ourselves without you doing anymore today. Besides, the boy is long gone by now."

"These Brilliants are smart for being newbies," Speed observed, clenching his left hand into a fist.

"They're certainly much stronger than the usual new Brilliants. Xylo senses this which is why he's put so much attention on them. It's also why he won't be pleased when he learns about this afternoon. Imagination, get rid of the gas and these masks. We need to go back inside, contact Thry, and return to the Triangle."

The men walked back into the store, and Juan watched the giant yellow doors close behind them. He got up and ran around the side of the building toward the sidewalk. His head was pounding, probably aftereffects of the gas, but that didn't stop him.

He crossed the street and headed toward the next block. Five minutes later, he entered Vanity's Look. Too exhausted to run anymore, he flopped down in a chair that was part of a back to school mannequin scene next to the entrance.

It was then that he realized he was visible, and that

his Vest had disappeared. But when had it disappeared? He had been in such a hurry to get to the store, he hadn't paid that much attention to it. He did notice, however, that the intense headache was almost gone, and he closed his eyes, wiping the sweat from his forehead.

"Juan, get out of there," Angelica's voice rang out.

He opened his eyes, and saw his sister walking toward him carrying a Vanity's Look bag.

"What are you doing? You're not supposed to sit in there, you nimrod."

Juan got up and tried not to step on one of the mannequin's dresses.

"I was just coming to pick you up," Angelica said.

Now it was decision time. Tell the truth or lie. "I didn't see anything I liked." He decided on deceit. The truth was too bizarre.

"That's a first," Angelica said sarcastically. "What were you doing? You're all sweaty."

"I ran over, trying to get some exercise," Juan said, attempting to sound casual.

"Okay . . ." Angelica shook her head. "Let's go home."

Chapter Ten
Juan's Room

Juan hardly ate any of his dinner. He barely talked to anyone and went to bed at an uncharacteristic eight o'clock, claiming that he was tired. And even though he was exhausted, he couldn't sleep. Nestled under his sheets, he stared at the digital clock on the dresser.

Two a.m.

He had gone over what had happened at the Hooked Nose so many times and what he would tell Samantha and George, that it was almost making him physically ill. Every creak and loud sound made him jump, and he had half a notion to turn invisible again as the wind howled outside. At any moment he expected the Dark-Vested men to burst through his bedroom window and take him away.

After staring at the ceiling another thirty minutes, he decided that he wouldn't be able to sleep in his own room tonight. And he knew he needed sleep. He grabbed his pillow and the top blanket from his bed, dragging them down the hallway to the last door on the left.

He opened it quietly, letting the light from the hallway in briefly before closing it. He felt his way over carefully to the base of Angelica's bed. He hadn't done this in years, but tonight, more than any other night, he was scared. This kind of scared, where the monsters are real, made what he was doing all the more important. He threw his pillow down first, then hunched over, pulling the blanket over himself before lying down on the soft carpet at the foot of his sister's bed.

Ever since he was five, he'd done this when he'd had a bad dream or gotten scared in the middle of the night. There was something about sleeping next to Angelica's bed that made him feel safe — safer than in his parents' room, because with them he would have to endure the speech about growing up and being brave. Angelica never asked questions or said things like that. When Juan finally closed his eyes, he was sound asleep in a matter of seconds.

It seemed like he'd slept about five minutes when he felt Angelica rocking him by the shoulder, telling him it was time to get up. He opened his eyes, which felt like they were on fire, and squinted up at her.

"You're late. You better hurry up," she said kindly.

Juan sat up slowly and ran his hand over his face, rubbing his eyes. He took a deep breath, grabbing his pillow and blanket before standing up. Angelica was seated in front of her dresser mirror, weaving her hair into small braids.

"Thanks," he said hoarsely.

"No problem," she replied with a smile.

No questions asked, no snide remarks about being afraid — just cool. That was his sister. That's why he loved her. That's why he trusted her.

He wolfed down a piece of toast and grabbed two dollars from his mother for lunch, barely making it to the bus stop on time. As soon as the bus pulled up to Eagle Crest, he got off quickly and found Samantha and George sitting on the bench where they had talked yesterday.

"Did you hear about it?" Samantha asked, as Juan eagerly approached them.

"Hear about what?" Juan said, throwing his backpack on the ground and sitting down on the grass in front of the bench.

"There was a robbery at the Hooked Nose yesterday. Someone came in and took all the money. A bunch of people said they were knocked out by some sort of strange animal," Samantha reported worriedly.

Juan felt a knot in his stomach. He hadn't seen an animal, but he'd heard noises, strange noises. "It was on the news?" he asked quietly.

"On the radio this morning," George added.

The knot was tightening, and it must have shown because Samantha and George picked up on it.

"What's the matter with you?" George asked, frowning.

"You're not going to believe me," Juan was whispering now, " but I was there. I saw what happened."

"You were where?"

"I was at the Hooked Nose when the robbery took place, and it wasn't a robbery. They were looking for me."

Samantha and George went white. "What do you mean? Who was looking for you?" Samantha asked, wide-eyed.

The bell rang and Juan grimaced, knowing that he didn't have time to tell them the whole story. "Can we meet tonight?"

George looked at Samantha apprehensively before turning back to Juan. "It's that bad?"

"Oh, you have no idea."

"Yeah, I can pick you guys up again and we can go to the Point."

"No," Juan chipped. "No way. I'm not leavin' my house. You come to my room at eleven. Bring Samantha, and I'll tell you everything."

Juan stood up and brushed off his backpack.

"Can't you just call and tell us after school?" Samantha

suggested.

"No. I'm not going to tell you this over the phone. They might have it bugged."

"What are you talking about?"

"Just be at my window at eleven tonight," Juan said sharply as they walked into school together, jockeying for position with other students in the hallway.

"Can't you just tell us?" Samantha persisted, trying to get Juan to give her more.

"No. Not here. Only at my house," he said seriously. "I don't know if we're being watched."

"What do you mean by that?" George begged, but Juan said nothing more.

George and Samantha had to be content to wait until eleven o'clock that night. For them, school went by slowly for two reasons. First, they were still living out their last day of in-house detention, and secondly, they couldn't imagine what Juan had to tell them.

Classes crawled along for Juan as well because he wanted — he needed — to tell his friends what had happened. Maybe Samantha's Vest would be able to make sense of it all. When it was finally time to get on the bus to go home, he told his best friends one last time to be at his window at eleven o'clock, no matter what.

When he got home, he grabbed a peanut butter and jelly sandwich, flopped down on the couch and fell asleep. It was six o'clock when his mother finally woke him for dinner.

Juan ate better that night, but not well enough to satisfy his mother.

"Are you feeling okay? What's the matter? You feel warm. You might be getting sick. You didn't eat well last night you know," she said periodically throughout the evening.

He played down the questions and comments the best he could and went to bed at nine o'clock with no intention of trying to sleep. He played back the events at the Hooked Nose over and over while stretched out on his bed, looking at the ceiling where he had pinned a poster of a large steelhead jumping out of the water.

At exactly eleven o'clock, Juan was helping Samantha and then George through the window. Both his friends were dressed warmly because the night was cold and windy, as it had been the night before. Samantha and George took off their coats and dropped them on the floor before sitting on Juan's bed expectantly. Juan slumped down beside them on the queen-sized bed.

"You want me to keep my Vest on so we have light?" George asked.

"No, go ahead and let it go, but Samantha, we're going to need yours," Juan whispered seriously.

In an instant, Samantha's Vest glowed brightly, illuminating the room. Juan took a deep breath, and began telling them everything that happened from the moment he first entered the Hooked Nose.

George and Samantha listened without a word as Juan described the screams and unconscious people, the gas, and the men in Dark Vests. He told them about escaping through the back doors and hearing what the men had said. Juan hoped that by listening with her Vest, Samantha would be able to answer at least some of the questions swimming around in his head.

"What is your Vest telling you about all this?" asked Juan after finishing his story.

"Give me a sec," Samantha said exhaustedly, like she had just run a long way. "It's so hard to believe. It sounds like a dream."

"It wasn't a dream! Believe me, I wish it had been because I'd be able to sleep better."

"This is gettin' freaky," said George, his voice cracking with fright. "What you just told us is that there are evil Vests, evil powers."

"That's right. I don't know if the Vests are evil, but the men wearing them are," Juan replied darkly.

"Well, you're right. Those men you saw are evil. They use their powers to do terrible things," Samantha added, her Vest pulsating with light. "But that's all I'm getting. I don't know what any of the other stuff you heard means."

"He mentioned Xylo. What is Xylo?"

Samantha closed her eyes and then shook her head. "I don't know."

"That's weird. Your Vest gives you some information but won't give you anything about this," Juan said dejectedly.

"It sounds like they've been spying on us for some time," George suggested. "That guy with the power of speed must've been who I saw that night I flew out. These guys have been trackin' our every move, I'll bet."

"They want us, I have no doubt," Juan said, standing up and beginning to pace. "I think they want our powers."

"I agree," Samantha added pensively.

"I wonder how many more people there are with Dark Vests," George reflected.

"Definitely more than we know about," Samantha answered quietly. "My Vest isn't exactly telling me that, but I sense it."

"I don't want this power anymore," Juan said suddenly. "I don't want to be afraid to sleep or worry that I'll turn invisible at any moment. At first I thought it was cool, but now I don't want any part of it."

"I don't think it's that easy, Juan. I don't think you can just cancel these powers, just like that," Samantha said, snapping her fingers. "We're stuck with them."

"I don't want to be stuck with them," Juan countered. "I just want my life back to normal."

"So what do we do?" George looked at both of them.

"We have to be careful. Don't go anywhere alone, and try not to use your Vest at all. But we have to make sure we're at the old barn at the fairgrounds by noon on September twenty-fifth so that we can find out more about all of this."

"Yeah, okay," Juan agreed.

George nodded. "We better go."

"Be careful," Juan warned as he slid the window open.

"Gotcha," George said, his Vest appearing over his coat.

Samantha's Vest was already gone before she put her coat on and carefully climbed out the window and onto George's back. "See you tomorrow at school."

Juan watched them drift off, shutting the window when they were out of sight. He picked up his pillow and blanket. Just like the night before, he walked quietly to Angelica's room and made himself comfortable at foot of her bed.

"You okay?" she whispered kindly as he put his head

down on the pillow.

"Yeah. I'm okay."

* * *

"Idiots!" Melt said furiously, staring at Strength, Speed, and Imagination. "First you fail with the girl, and now you're telling me you can't even catch the boy?"

"I don't know how she could have escaped the dinosaurs I released, Melt," Imagination said, attempting to defend himself.

"And I already told you the boy was invisible," Strength argued.

"These are kids! And had you not forgotten about the back doors, you would've had the boy. Don't you ever wonder where they unload the goods from the trucks!" Melt spat. "Now I have to go and tell Xylo of yet another failure. He will not be pleased!"

"We can go and take them out. . . ." Strength started, but Melt raised his hand.

"You're not going to do anything until the day they are to meet their Envoys in that barn at the fairgrounds. Until then, you'll remain in the Triangle. Is that understood?"

Strength gritted his teeth angrily but said nothing, staring into Melt's cold eyes.

"Is that understood, all of you?"

The three men nodded.

"I'm warning you though, Strength. If you fail one more time with this, I will melt you to nothing."

"Never send a man to do a woman's job," came the crackly voice of Thry.

"Shut up, Thry!" Strength bellowed.

"You're worthless, Strength. Why you haven't been disposed of already is a mystery to me."

"I'm warning you, old hag, I'll crush your neck into a thousand pieces."

"There'll be no crushing today," Melt interrupted. "Thry, take these three back to the Triangle, and then come back and pick me up. We need to meet with Xylo."

"Yes, Melt," the old woman said as she led Strength, Speed, and Imagination through the black syrupy porthole shimmering to their left. "I shall return quickly."

Chapter Eleven
The Dance

Just as they had the previous morning, Samantha, George, and Juan met at the bench before school officially started. Not one of them had gotten a good night's sleep, and it showed. Large, puffy bags drooped down under their eyes, and they took turns yawning as they talked. The conversation was the same as it had been the last few days.

"We need to make sure that we all get to the fairgrounds by noon on the twenty-fifth," Samantha said quietly as other students passed by.

"Well, what about this," Juan proposed. "Me and George can spend the night at your house Friday night, the twenty-fourth."

"The night of the fall dance?" Samantha asked.

"Right. George and I will stay at your house, and maybe your brother can drive us to the fair in the morning. It opens at ten, so we might as well get there early and play around before we go to the old barn."

"That might work." George nodded. "I'm not

grounded after this weekend, so I'll probably be able to do it. You think your parents will let us?"

"Probably," Samantha said.

"It's not like we haven't done it before," Juan added. "Just tell them we want to go to the fair together."

"Okay . . . yeah, that should work," agreed Samantha.

The bell rang and they joined the other students in the crowded hallway. Samantha split up with Juan and George, moving with the flow of traffic along the left side of the hall. She made it to her top locker and put in the combination. The lock snapped open, and she swung the door out slowly. She stared incredulously for a long time and whispered, "What is that?"

Everything in the locker — her clothes, her books, her pencils and pens — everything was covered in what looked like raw egg. She took out one of the pencils and held it up as it dripped yolk on the floor.

Mariah Daily, whose locker was below Samantha's, looked up in disgust, having almost been hit by the drippy mess.

"What is that?" Mariah asked, standing up and looking inside Samantha's locker.

"It looks like egg," Samantha answered, afraid to touch anything.

"But how could someone get egg in there?" Mariah

wondered, still looking disgusted.

"I don't know," Samantha said irritably. "It's ruined all of my books."

She took out her English text saturated with yolk.

"Well, what happened here?" came Paul's voice from behind. "Ooh, yuck! What is that?"

Samantha swung around and stared at Paul, who was smiling so broadly she couldn't see his eyes.

"You did this!" she said sharply.

Paul let out a fake laugh. "Now, how could I do that? Looks like someone crushed a little egg in your locker there. The only way someone could do that is if they knew your combination."

Samantha went scarlet. Mariah looked at Paul with the same disgust she had shown for the egg in Samantha's locker.

"Paul, you did it. It's so obvious. You're so gross," Mariah said and kicked her locker shut before walking away. "Creep."

"It was you! I know it!" Samantha said, pointing a finger accusingly at Paul.

"Tough to say who it is, huh — can't prove it or anything, so it looks like you're stuck. Stuck," he said and laughed at his own joke. "Love the pun . . . get it . . . stuck."

"Paul. . . ." Samantha breathed heavily, her fists clenched.

Paul leaned in and whispered, "You shouldn't have turned me down for the dance, and you shouldn't have kicked me. Now look what's happened. Tut, tut." Paul waved his finger reprovingly. "Thought you were smarter than that."

And he strode off giggling.

Samantha was so angry she couldn't find the right words to respond. Her face was the color of a ripe tomato. She wanted to tell a teacher or her counselor that Paul had cracked eggs inside her locker, but he was right. She had no proof, and without some sort of evidence the school wouldn't do anything.

She was very late to her first-period class, but Mr. Dorn didn't want to hear about it as he wrote up a tardy slip. She had managed to clean up most of her books, but many of the pages were still stuck together. First day out of in-house detention, and she was late and had egg everywhere — not a great start.

The next three periods went by quickly, not because she was having a particularly good day, but because it was refreshing to actually be in class instead of sitting at a table by herself doing menial assignments.

At noon, Samantha headed for the large cafeteria which hosted a variety of small booths offering everything from pizza to candy bars. Samantha took two dollars from her pocket and checked the lunch menu. Spaghetti and meatballs didn't look appetizing. She decided on a soda, a package of peanut butter cookies, and a mini pizza.

She usually sat with Kristina and her other friends at a back table, but today she went to find George and Juan, who were sitting alone at a table next to the candy booth.

"What are you doing?" Juan asked, his mouth full of Milky Way.

"I'm sittin' here with you guys, if that's okay," Samantha said with a smile as she sat down at the table.

"You don't usually sit with us," George said, using a napkin to wipe the spaghetti from his mouth.

"Yeah, so . . ." Samantha said, opening up her bag of cookies.

"I don't know — you just usually sit with Kristina and the other girls."

"Well, I wanted to sit with you and tell you what Paul did to my locker."

Samantha took a bite of her cookie.

"What did he do?" Juan asked.

"I think he got my combination somehow and broke a bunch of eggs in the locker. There's yolk everywhere."

"Egg?" George said disgustedly.

"Egg — all over my books, my pens, my clothes . . .

over everything."

"Sick," Juan said, stuffing the rest of the candy bar into his mouth.

"How do you know it was Paul? Did you use your Vest?" asked George, returning to his spaghetti.

"No, but he just about admitted it to me this morning. He said that I should have agreed to go to the dance with him, and that I shouldn't have kicked him."

Samantha took another bite.

George smiled. "Egg, huh?"

"It's not funny. Most of the pages in the books stick together."

"The perfect excuse for not doing homework, and it'd actually be true. 'Please, teacher, please,'" Juan said in an overly excited, high pitched voice, "'you can't give me a F because I couldn't get the book open.'"

George laughed aloud, but Samantha was stone-faced. "You wouldn't be laughing if they were your books and you had to pay for them at the end of the year."

"Oh, don't worry about it," Juan said, waving his hand nonchalantly. "The guy just wants to go to the dance with you."

"The guy's an idiot," Samantha retorted.

"So what's that say about you?" George sneered.

"Oh, okay. Who have you asked to go?" she snapped,

hoping to change the direction of the conversation.

This shut them both up.

"Thought so. Neither of you have asked anyone to the dance, have you?"

"It's not a dance like that. We're not in high school. It's just a school dance, but you act like it's supposed to be all formal and stuff," George said defensively.

"I do not think it's suppose to be formal, George. It would be nice to go with someone, though. And I know a lot of guys that have asked girls to go."

"Well, there's always Paul," Juan said, unable to keep the laughter out of his voice.

"Anyway," Samantha said in a change-the-subject voice, "I really came over to talk about getting Paul, and I think I have a plan."

"Uh oh. Another plan?" Juan took a drink of Pepsi. "Remember your plan last year that nearly got us expelled?"

Samantha drew a blank.

"C'mon. Remember? The kitchen . . . lunchtime."

"Oh, well . . . that was different."

"Yeah, right. You had us spying in the kitchen, trying to expose the cooks for not wearing gloves, remember? And George and I ended up getting locked in the freakin' freezer for a half hour just so you could do some stupid editorial in the lame school newspaper," cried Juan, still bitter about the frosty ordeal. "'Bring the camera and sneak in the back before lunch and take pictures. . . .'" he said in a high voice meant to imitate Samantha's. "Almost froze to death, for God's sake."

"Okay, okay. So it wasn't a good plan, but this one's better. Won't you at least hear me out?"

Juan looked at George and sighed. "We'll listen," he said, "but that doesn't mean we're going along with it."

"Fine," Samantha said, sitting up straighter and leaning over the table. "It starts at the dance. . . ."

* * *

The days leading up to the fall dance passed quickly. Classes were in full swing, and Eagle Crest Middle School was living up to its reputation of barraging students with homework, which was a good thing because, at least most of the time, it kept Samantha's, George's, and Juan's minds somewhat off their powers and the fright of being attacked by men in Dark Vests or dinosaur-like creatures. At night, however, it was difficult to avoid wondering how long it would be before another attack occurred.

Samantha used her Vest every night, asking the same basic questions about the men with Dark Vests — who were they? Where did they come from? How did they get their powers? But it was futile because she came up blank. What good was a Vest of Knowledge if the information she needed wasn't available? She had been faithful in not using it for homework and tests, although she had been tempted to do so on the brutal pre-algebra test she had taken on Wednesday.

Juan was still sleeping at the foot of Angelica's bed, and she didn't question it. He tried sleeping in his own room a few times, but the vision of being captured by evil men won out and each night found him back on Angelica's floor.

Friday, September twenty-fourth arrived, and the three of them had convinced their parents that they should all spend the night at Samantha's. That had been the easy part; getting Samantha's older brother to agree to drop them off at the fair on his way to work was the tough part. Eventually Brian caved, but only if Samantha paid him five dollars, which she thought was ludicrous. After all, he was her brother.

At seven o'clock in the evening, having been dropped off for the dance by Samantha's dad, they made their way toward the gym doors. George and Juan wore jeans, T-shirts, and tennis shoes — standard school attire. Samantha, on the contrary was wearing a dress that definitely wasn't standard for school. It was tight fitting and coupled with her flowing, dark hair, made her look eighteen. Both boys had to admit she looked simply beautiful.

"You look good," Juan said, sounding surprised that Samantha could look so different than she did at school.

"You think you might be overdressed?" George wondered, looking her up and down with raised eyebrows as they approached the blue doors leading into the gym.

"Maybe you're underdressed," she retorted.

George's thought of Samantha being overdressed was erased as soon as he entered the loud gymnasium. All the girls were wearing outfits similar to Samantha's, and the boys, George was relieved to see, looked just like he and Juan did.

"I'm going over with Kristina. I'll see you guys later and remember . . ."

"Yeah, yeah," George and Juan said in unison, as they watched her walk over to her friend's table.

"This is gonna be boring," Juan said, motioning to a small white table near the wall.

Round tables surrounded by white plastic patio chairs were placed around the center of the gym. A glistening disco ball that shot light everywhere on the floor and off the walls. A long picnic-like table loaded with junk food, salads, and a huge punch bowl had been set up under one of the basketball hoops.

The place was packed with students but not surprisingly, very few of them were actually dancing. Most of the girls were hanging out near the dance floor, standing and chatting together in groups. The guys were either at the patio tables or getting food.

"It's not like we're going to dance," Juan said, as he and George sat down.

"Yeah," George agreed.

They sat in silence for awhile, watching Nigel Jeris and Beth Winters dance, if you could call it that. Mostly they just stood still and moved their arms. Eventually, more and more students filtered out onto the center area of the floor.

Teachers were spread throughout the gym, walking around and talking pleasantly with students making sure that everything was under control. Juan got up and looked at his watch.

"Want some punch?" he asked George, who seemed to be focusing on the floor in some kind of stupor. "Yo, George."

George shook his head. "Huh? Yeah, sure."

"You okay?"

"Fine. Just thinkin'."

"That was obvious. Be right back."

George looked back down at the floor and was about to resume his thoughts about how Samantha's plan was actually going to work, when he felt someone tap him on the shoulder. He turned and, for a moment, thought he was dreaming because standing next to him, looking absolutely gorgeous, was Aerial Sampson, a seventh-grader with the most spectacular blond hair he had ever seen.

"Hi, George," she said sweetly.

George's heart melted. His mouth suddenly went very dry.

"Ah . . . hi . . ." he stammered.

This was the first time he had ever really spoken to Aerial. He stared at her all the time in English class because she was Mrs. Gipson's assistant, but he had never said anything to her.

"Do you want to dance?" Aerial asked.

George's hand shook, and he thought for a moment he might faint. 'Say something, you moron,' he thought. "Sure."

He got up quickly, in fact so quickly that he slammed his knee into the front of the table. Aerial looked concerned, but George sucked in the pain, gave a nod toward the center of the gym, and hobbled into the crowd of kids.

Dancing was something that George rarely did, but when he did, he did it alone. He had never imagined that he would be dancing with Aerial Sampson, of all people. The music was loud and there were kids everywhere, which made

George feel more comfortable knowing that he was just an-other body amidst all the others. But it also made him uncom-fortable because people could see that he didn't know what he was doing.

The music was fast with a strong beat, and as Aerial began moving, George knew he would have to move as well or look like a complete idiot, in which case Aerial would never ask him to dance again. Surprisingly, he found it wasn't diffi-cult at all, and a minute into the song he was smiling, not so much because he was with Aerial but because he found that he actually could dance.

As he moved around, he glanced over at the table where Juan stood, absolutely dumbstruck, holding a plastic cup and staring agape at his friend.

"You see, Juan —" Samantha said, walking up and taking the cup from his right hand.

"What's he doing?" Juan asked in amazement.

Samantha took George's empty seat. "It looks like he's dancing."

"Yeah, but with . . . with . . ."

"Aerial Sampson."

"Yeah."

"So, what's the big deal?"

"The big deal?" Juan said incredulously, still standing

and holding his cup of punch. "She's a seventh-grader."

"So?"

Samantha took a sip of punch.

"But he doesn't know how to dance," Juan said, finally sitting down.

"Looks like he's doing okay to me," Samantha said, finishing her punch in two large gulps.

"Hmmm."

"Remember. As soon as you see Paul go for the bathroom . . . "

"I know. I'll get George. But you've got the easy part —you don't even do anything."

"Can't. I don't have the power of invisibility," she said smugly.

"Funny." Juan faked a smile.

"Make sure you're not seen turning . . ."

"Don't worry — Mom."

"Just be sure you come and get me after you do it," Samantha said, patting him on the shoulder and walking away.

When the song ended, to Juan's disbelief George stayed out on the dance floor with Aerial and danced the next two songs before returning to the table. Juan was busy looking across the gym toward Paul who was standing and talking with Dean

Farrell, an eighth-grader.

"Can you believe it?" George said blissfully. "I was dancing with Aerial Sampson. She actually asked me to dance, buddy."

Juan shook his head and smiled. "I almost collapsed when I saw you out on the floor with her. You get so lucky."

"She just came up, tapped me on the shoulder, and asked me if I wanted to dance. Yeah, baby."

George turned and scanned the tables and groups of girls before finally finding Aerial, who was looking at him, pointing and talking with three other girls. George waved and turned back to Juan who was standing and looking across the center of dancers toward Paul.

George stood up next to him.

"Is he going?" George asked.

"Yeah, I think," Juan replied, focused. "Come on."

George followed Juan around the group of dancers, toward the hallway leading to the bathrooms. They got to the hall just in time to see Paul enter the boys' bathroom. George glanced behind him and noticed that, besides the kids sitting along the wall talking and paying no attention to him, the hallway was empty. George was about to tell Juan it was all clear, but Juan had already gone invisible, so George had no idea where he was.

"Juan, you there?" George whispered, continuing to walk toward the bathroom.

"Yeah," Juan whispered. "Okay, you watch the door. Here we go."

To Juan, everything looked just as it did when he was visible, except for the brilliant glow coming from his Vest. He pushed the bathroom door open and could sense George at his heels. Samantha's plan would work more effectively if Paul was the only one in the bathroom.

George was standing still, his back propped against the door. He leaned against it, using the facing wall to brace his feet so that if anyone happened to wander in, he could hold the door shut, at least for a few seconds. His heart was racing. The euphoria of dancing with Aerial had worn off considerably.

Juan rounded the corner stealthily and there was Paul, standing in front of the large mirror, muttering things to himself as he checked his teeth for tiny bits of food. Juan scanned the rest of the bathroom. He didn't see anyone else. He ducked down and checked for feet under the stalls.

Nothing.

All clear.

Juan took a quiet, deep breath, and then he did it. He charged at Paul with all his might, crossed his arms and lowered his shoulder like they taught him at football camp last summer, bowling into an unsuspecting Paul.

The sudden jolt sent the boy into the air, his teeth slamming down on his lip as he skidded across the tile floor. Blood poured from his mouth and tears welled up in his eyes. He looked around the room in sheer terror. There was nothing there but . . . but . . . something had just slammed him to the ground. He got to his knees and was about to stand up, when he heard a voice in front of him say, "Paul Hertzinger."

George was laughing hard, but silently. He heard Paul hit the floor. Now the way Juan was speaking, in an uncharacteristically low tone, made George want to bust open. He wondered how Juan was doing it without laughing.

"Who are you?" Paul shrieked, looking frantic.

"Stay where you are and listen to me," Juan ordered, actually sounding menacing.

Drama paid off, George thought.

"I am the ghost of Eagle Crest, and I have been watching you, Paul. You have been picking on others, hurting others. Haven't you, Paul?"

"No, no," Paul lied, as blood poured down his chin onto his white shirt.

"Don't lie to the ghost of Eagle Crest!" Juan shouted.

George could hear Paul whimper like a wounded dog.

"Okay. Okay. Yeah, I've picked on some kids,"

"Never again, you understand me! Never! If I see you, and believe me I can see you all the time," Juan said, now immersed in his part, "I will hunt you down, and I will come for you!"

Paul was in a full, heaving cry, and for a moment, however brief, Juan felt sorry for him because, at that point he realized Paul was really a coward.

"I will go and leave you for now."

This was George's cue. He turned and opened the bathroom door quickly, making his exit as quietly as possible. He walked as casually as he could down the hallway and back into the gym toward the table. He'd just sat down and looked over toward the hallway when Paul came bursting into the gym, shouting like a madman.

"A ghost! There's a ghost in . . . in . . . the . . . bathroom!"

Blood still ran profusely from his cut lip, and his stained white shirt made it look as if he'd been severely injured. Maybe it was the loud music, maybe it was the fact that nobody ever took Paul seriously, but for whatever reason, no one besides Mrs. Dibble paid any attention to him.

Mrs. Dibble, the home economics teacher, patted him on the head like a dog and led him over to the water fountain in the corner of the gym to get his lip cleaned up. George was now laughing out loud. There was no sense in being silent. Just then, Juan emerged from the hallway and made his way over to the table, smiling mischievously.

"You should've seen his face," Juan laughed, pulling up a chair. "Where'd he go?"

"I think Dibble took him to the office to get him cleaned up. He had blood everywhere."

"Yeah, I slammed him pretty hard."

"Would have loved to have seen it."

"Oh, he was freaked. You know what's gonna happen now, don't you?" Juan asked with a wry smile. "He's gonna tell the whole school, and you watch, I'll bet there's a rumor by Monday that there's a ghost in the school."

Samantha rushed over. "I saw Mrs. Dibble taking Paul out of the gym. Did it work?"

Juan nodded. "Your plan worked, Manthers. I got him good. He's so scared. I doubt he'll bug you anymore."

Samantha shook her fist in vindication. "Yes! I told you!"

"Don't start," George said, tersely. "It only worked because there wasn't anyone else in the bathroom, and no one tried to come in while Juan was scaring him. We just got lucky."

"He got what he deserved."

"I think he got a little more than he deserved," Juan said honestly. "He was really scared, Manthers."

This seemed to sober Samantha a bit. She stopped laughing and took a seat next to them. "That will be the last time we'll do that," she said, now much quieter.

"At least to him," joked George. "Don't worry, he'll get over it."

Chapter Twelve
The Fair

By the time Samantha's dad picked them up from the dance, George, Samantha, and Juan were ready to call it a night. Samantha had danced with just about every guy in sixth grade, and George had spent what was left of the dance after the bathroom caper with Aerial, dancing or talking at a table of their own.

Meanwhile, Juan had drunk enough fruit punch to irrigate a small orchard. He only danced twice. Once with Rozi Pudderbacher, a sixth-grader who towered a good five inches over him, and once with Susan Weathers, a thin girl who danced like a chicken. But all in all, it'd been fun.

George and Juan changed into their pajamas and curled up in their sleeping bags in the dimly lit living room. Although there was a certain need to talk about the coming morning, it was useless since Samantha's bedroom was upstairs. Neither had difficulty going to sleep. For the first time since the events in the Hooked Nose, Juan hadn't thought about

Dark-Vested men attacking him as he slept.

Both boys were awakened the next morning by Samantha's mother calling their names for breakfast. Juan stretched and yawned while George leaned forward, sat up, and rubbed his eyes.

"I couldda slept another couple hours," George said sleepily.

"Yeah," Juan grunted, climbing out of his sleeping bag and rubbing his neck.

By the time they had changed, brushed their teeth, and washed up, breakfast was ready. The whole house was filled with the tantalizing smells of eggs, bacon, and pancakes, compliments of Mrs. Banks.

The boys had spent enough nights at the Banks's house to know that Samantha's mom could cook. By the time she put everything out, the table was so full it was tough to squeeze in the plates. First was the fruit — freshly cut cantaloupe and watermelon — along with steaming hot bacon and eggs, followed by a gargantuan stack of pancakes the size of hubcaps.

Juan wondered as he poured the thick homemade syrup over two of his cakes how on earth the family stayed so skinny. There was so much food on the table it was a wonder the whole lot of them weren't elephant-sized. The pancakes were the best, and Juan took his time, savoring each bite.

No one said much during breakfast, partly because Samantha, George, and Juan couldn't discuss what they wanted to. So instead, they ate breakfast quietly as Mrs. Banks prepared the last of the pancakes.

It wasn't until George was finishing his last bite of scrambled egg that Brian came into the kitchen looking rushed. He took five pieces of bacon from the pile on the plate and made his way to the refrigerator, pulling out a liter of apple juice.

"Have to get going, Mom," he said quickly.

"Don't forget Sam and her friends," his mother said, finally sitting down at the table to eat.

"I know. Come on you guys."

"You have money?" Mrs. Banks asked, looking at Juan and George.

"Yes," Juan said.

George nodded.

"Okay, have fun."

"What about my money?" Samantha asked sarcastically, sticking out her hand.

Mrs. Banks slapped it away playfully. "Good try, but you already have yours. Now get outta here."

Samantha smiled, and she followed Brian, Juan, and

George out the front door and into the four-door van. She didn't particularly enjoy riding with Brian. He didn't exactly drive like her parents, even when he had to use the family van. Samantha's father was a strict law-abiding citizen when it came to road speed, but her brother was just the opposite.

It only took Brian eight minutes to get to the fairgrounds; it would've taken his father fifteen. The three of them got out quickly because Brian had parked illegally in front of a fire hydrant.

"I'll pick you up here," Brian said before pulling away so fast the tires squealed and smoked.

"Does he always drive like that?" George asked, shaking his head.

"Always," Samantha replied.

"That was a little scary, especially when he turned that corner too fast and almost hit that old guy and his dog," Juan said, a tinge of fear in his voice.

"He always waits until the last minute to go anywhere and then speeds to get there. Like work. I'll bet he's got to be in by ten and . . ." Samantha said, glancing at her watch, "it looks like he's got about five minutes to get there on time."

"C'mon, let's go in. We only have a couple of hours before we meet." Juan slapped George on the back and led him and Samantha to Gate Two where they handed the ticket vendor enough money for admission and twenty tickets to be used for just about everything from food to rides.

It was the last weekend of the fair, and like every year, the place was jam-packed with people going here and there like a colony of ants.

"Let's hit the Insane Spinner!" George rubbed his hands together eagerly before pointing to the large missile-like structure about fifty yards away.

"No way. Not this year," Juan said, stopping and pointing at George accusingly. "You remember what happened last year? I went on that stupid thing and ended up yakkin'. No, thanks. You two go."

George was laughing as Samantha tried to coax Juan to join them.

"Come on, Juan. It won't be as bad as you think the second time around."

"How do you know?"

"The second time is always better," Samantha said smoothly.

Juan wasn't biting. "No, you guys go. I'm hittin' the arcade. Come get me when you're done."

"Okay," Samantha said, slowly. "But you're going to miss out."

"I don't think so," Juan said, waving his hand in front

of him.

"You're sure?" George asked a final time.

"I'm sure. Go ahead."

George and Samantha made their way toward the rides while Juan headed in the opposite direction in search of the arcade tent. For George and Samantha an hour passed by quickly. They rode the Insane Spinner — twice — the Gravratron, the Yo-Yo, the Mixelplix, and a new ride called Drop Your Stomach. When they got off that one, they knew how it got its name.

Juan's hour passed just as quickly. He had concentrated on Ultra Pinball, the combination of a classic pinball game along with a screen that you had to watch in order to continue play. It had taken him ten bucks worth of tokens, but by the time George and Samantha tapped him on the shoulder, he had the high score.

"This game rocks," he said, admiring his name on the high scores display.

"How long have you been playing?" asked George, sounding impressed as he stared at Juan's name. Samantha didn't seem to care.

"Just about the whole time," Juan said proudly.

"We've got about fifty minutes before we're suppose to meet at the barn," Samantha said, looking at her watch.

"What do you want to do?" George asked.

"Let's go to the game booths. Maybe I'll actually be able to win something this year," Samantha mumbled as she walked out of the large tent with George and Juan following.

* * *

The old barn at the end of the fairgrounds hadn't been used for three years, and why the fair hadn't destroyed it was anyone's guess. It had been one of the original buildings when the fair opened years ago, but it had lost its usefulness, and now was more of an eyesore than anything else. Hardly anyone ever ventured into it, which was one of the reasons the Will had chosen it for the meeting place of the new Brilliants and their Envoys.

"Good spot," Julian said, appearing in a flash of light.

"Not bad," Jannick answered, surveying the ground that was littered with old hay.

Both boys were fourteen years old, and nearly identical in height and weight. Their features, however, were much different. Julian was a straight-haired, thick-faced boy, with sunken in cheeks. Jannick's hair was thick and red, and his face looked a lot like a puffy blowfish. His cheeks were like miniature balloons that sandwiched his lips into a slight pucker. His face was scattered with freckles that went along nicely with his green eyes.

In a brilliant explosion of golden light, a third boy appeared. He was much taller than the other two. Luis was seventeen and built like a football player with a short, stocky neck and wide shoulders. His black hair was hidden by a Florida Gators baseball cap with the bill pulled over his forehead so tight it was tough to see his hazel eyes.

Another bright explosion of light followed almost immediately after Luis. It was Jazmin, the beautiful fifteen-year old girl who had the Gift of Transport. She had smooth, radiant skin with long, golden locks of hair that were finely braided and fell to her hips. Her eyes were an icy blue, and her lips were full and curved.

All four were wearing bright Vests of Light.

"Are you sure you don't want me to stay?" Jazmin asked, looking cautiously around the barn.

"No need," said Luis easily. "There's no sense in you staying while we brief them. Besides, you said that Evenina needed you back at the Lighthouse, so just go. We're gonna be here awhile. We'll buzz you when we need you."

"You're sure?"

"Go."

"Okay."

In a circular blast of light, she disappeared.

The barn was silent as the three boys stood quietly scanning the area and listening carefully.

"Looks clear," Julian finally said, stepping forward.

Neither Luis nor Jannick heard Julian as he moved because he had the Gift of Stealth. His power gave him the ability to become silent, so that when he walked, jumped, climbed, or did anything besides talk, it couldn't be heard.

Luis's Vest gave him the power of repulsion — the unique Gift allowed him to repulse or throw back objects from very long distances. He had been given that Gift when he had found an old Chest atop a roof he was helping his father repair. He'd discovered it while his father had gone to the store, leaving him alone on the rooftop replacing shingles. From that moment on, as with most of those who open a Chest of Light, his life was forever changed.

Jannick's Gift of Sight came when he was swimming along the beach in North Carolina late one summer afternoon. Every August his family vacationed there, and he loved swimming. His family was much further along the beach that day when he'd discovered the Chest, half-buried in the sand and decided to open it.

When he did, he knew he'd done something that would change his life — especially when he was struck by a bolt of light and heard the words, "To you, the Gift of Sight."

It had taken him only a few seconds to realize what the voice had meant, because he suddenly found that he could focus on and see objects from incredible distances. Seashells on the beach two thousand yards away were as clear as if he were holding them in his hands. His parents, who had just been small figures in the distance, looked like they were standing next to him. He not only could see long distances, he could zoom in just as easily and effectively as any camera or telescope.

"You think they're nervous?" Julian asked, sitting down on what was left of a decaying bail of hay.

"Oh, yeah. I was when I first met the Brilliants," Luis said, putting his hands in the pockets of his jeans.

"Who greeted you?" asked Julian curiously.

"The Maker."

"The Maker greeted you?" Julian asked, wide-eyed.

"Yeah," Luis smiled. "Hard to believe, huh? Who met you?"

"Bess," Julian replied solemnly.

"Really?" Jannick came into the conversation.

"She was really sweet."

Jannick and Luis nodded, and for a moment there was dedicated silence.

"What about you?" Luis asked, looking at Jannick.

"You don't know?" Jannick seemed astonished.

"No. Who?"

"Malavax," Jannick said, a tone of disgust in his voice.

"Malavax? Are you serious?" Luis asked, taking his hands out of his pockets. "Malavax? Freakin' Malavax greeted you?"

"Yes. Man, I thought everyone knew that."

"No," Luis said, amazed. "I never knew she was an Envoy before she turned."

"Oh yeah. She was cool. I liked her."

"I bet you did. Everyone does. She's gorgeous, but still, to be greeted by her. Whew, buddy. I had no idea," Luis said, putting his hand on Jannick's shoulder.

"Me neither," Julian added sympathetically.

"She never tried to get me though," Jannick said, looking above him at the loft, reflecting on her image.

"Still . . . Malavax. . . ." Luis couldn't help himself.

Luis, Jannick, nor Julian didn't have time to react to what happened next. Perhaps if they'd had some sort of warning that danger was approaching, they could've been ready. . . .

Luis saw them first and was the first one to be attacked. He screamed as he saw the first hideous looking dinosaur approach, galloping wildly on two legs, its claws outstretched, but he wasn't quick enough to get out of the way. The creature jumped into the air and plunged onto him, all of its weight bearing down on his chest. Even though he was a stout football player, the force of the creature was too much. He tried to repulse the ugly thing off him, but couldn't use his power quickly enough, and his last image was that of the creature lunging at his neck.

Jannick had turned in time to avoid another dinosaur as it hurled itself at him. He rolled and saw an old pitchfork buried under a clump of hay. He reached down and brought it up as the creature turned and rushed forward. He could sense Julian to his right, struggling with another creature. That's when he heard the terrible ripping sound.

Jannick stood his ground as the creature charged. It leapt into the air, and he drove the pitchfork into its body. The creature let out an ear-piercing scream and fell to the ground flailing, as he shoved the tool further into its torso.

Suddenly, a sharp pain shot through his back and forced him to the ground, face first. Another sharp pain, and this seemed to be going deeper into this shoulder than the last one. He turned his head and saw Julian's lifeless eyes staring at him. It was the last thing that Jannick saw before another shooting pain pierced his body and everything went white.

"Nice," Strength said, the last one to climb through a large opening in the decaying barn wall. "Got to love your power, Imag."

"Thank you," Imagination said gloatingly, watching the last of the dinosaurs climb off Jannick's dead body.

In a swoosh of his hand, the creatures vanished, leaving the barn in eerie silence.

Strength let out a long, low, ugly laugh. "This couldn't have worked more perfectly. The Brilliants are so easy to predict. Of course, the Envoys would be here early, in case the new Vests arrived early. This was all too easy."

"About time it was this easy," Speed said, standing next to Strength. "After all we had to take from Melt. He's going to be pleased."

"Indeed," Strength said, smiling.

Imagination stepped closer to the lifeless bodies on the ground. "What should we do with them?"

"Leave them — scare the new Vests when they come in. Just be ready with those dinosaurs and remember — no killing — at least not yet."

"Understood." Imagination grinned wickedly. "This is working out perfectly. It will not be long until we have captured all the Brilliants. Then, no one will be left to stand in our way."

* * *

"We've played enough games, Samantha. Why are we stopping at this booth?" George asked impatiently, looking down at his watch. "We only have five minutes before we're supposed to meet at the old barn. It's going to take that long to walk over there."

Samantha nodded. "I know. This won't take long, I promise."

She walked to the front of the booth. In the center were hundreds of green glass bottles, and standing behind the small counter was one of the most disgusting men Samantha had ever seen.

Hair grew everywhere along his face, from the top of his cheeks all the way down to the middle of his neck. It looked like he hadn't shaved for years. His eyes were barely visible, but from what Samantha could see, they were narrow and brown. The man was wearing a shirt that was three sizes too small for him, and his potbelly protruded out so far that the shirt couldn't cover his pierced and infected belly button. He leered at her, exposing his two chipped, yellow front teeth.

"So you want to play, do you?" the man asked in a nasally voice.

Samantha nodded, and as she did, a brilliant Vest wrapped around her upper body.

"What are you doing?" Juan asked in a hush.

"Samantha!" George whispered harshly standing next to her.

"I'm playing," Samantha answered evenly and gave the man a dollar.

"You know how to play?" the man asked impatiently.

"No," Samantha replied flatly.

"Dumb kid," the man grumbled, reaching under the lip of the counter and pulling out three large red rings.

"You see these rings?"

"Duh," answered Samantha sardonically.

The man paused, not quite sure how to respond. He finally decided to continue. "You throw the rings and get them to go around the neck of the bottles. It's easy."

"Really?"

"Yes."

"Then show me. Demonstrate," Samantha ordered.

"What?" The man looked surprised.

"Yeah, if it's so easy, you throw the rings around the bottles."

A small group of kids were beginning to gather around, and it was obvious this was the most attention the potbellied man had received in a long time because he straightened up, puffed out his chest, and threw the first ring.

It slid easily around the neck of one of the bottles.

The small crowd that had gathered cheered. The man looked at Samantha and gave her an I'd-like-to-see-you-do-that smile. He turned and threw the second ring. Easy fit. He launched the third ring, and it too slid around the neck of another bottle without any problem. The man went over to the bottles and proudly picked up his rings, then turned to face Samantha again.

"You see, it's easy. Now, your turn." He reached below the counter again and withdrew three green rings, handing them to Samantha. She refused to take them.

"No, I want the red rings in your other hand," she said, pointing to his left hand.

"What?"

"Those rings — there in your other hand. I want those."

"You have your own," the man said huffily, shoving the three red rings under the counter.

"No, I want to use the red rings."

"You have your own." Potbellied man was becoming

frustrated.

George and Juan had forgotten about the time and the fact that they were late. They watched Samantha intensely.

"No, I don't want to use those." Samantha pointed to the green rings on the counter. "I want to use yours. You know why?"

"No. Why?"

"Because yours are different. The red rings are bigger than these green ones, and the red ones fit easily around the bottles so you don't have to make the perfect throw. The rings you're trying to give me are so much smaller that it's almost impossible to get them around the bottles. Now, I want to use your rings!"

The crowd began to shout at the man, who stood there trying to figure out how Samantha knew what only he was supposed to know.

"Give her the rings! Give her the rings!" the crowd chanted.

The man pulled out the red rings again and slammed them into Samantha's outstretched hand.

"Here," he sneered. "Good luck. You won't get all three."

"Uh huh," Samantha said briskly.

She took the first ring, aimed, and threw it. It slid

easily around one of the bottles. The man looked positively outraged. She threw the next one — a perfect fit. Samantha smiled.

"You're right. It's so easy."

And with that, she tossed the third ring and it, like the previous two, wrapped around the neck of one of the bottles.

She had won.

Potbellied man was livid. For a moment, George thought he was going to attack Samantha, but apparently the yelling and screaming crowd made him change his mind. Samantha jumped up on the counter, got on her tiptoes and grabbed the large pink elephant that hung prominently in front.

"I believe I get my choice," she said arrogantly.

The man stared at her as the crowd, made up of mostly children, clambered forward, holding out one-dollar bills and demanding to use the red rings Samantha had used. Samantha giggled, and looked at the elephant with great satisfaction.

"What did you just do?" George asked, flabbergasted as the three of them left the booth and headed toward the old barn that loomed in the distance.

"I'm smart, but I just needed to be a little smarter,"

Samantha said with a grin.

Juan and George had to laugh. In all the years they'd know Samantha they'd never seen her act so pretentiously, so boldly, unless George counted the negative number argument she'd had with Mr. Dorn.

Chapter Thirteen
The Robe

"This place is creepy," Juan said, leading Samantha and George through the large opening in the barn wall.

The sun had poked out from behind the clouds and was now shooting bright rays of light through the holes in the decaying roof, casting black shadows everywhere. The contrasting light and dark made it difficult to see the bodies of Luis, Jannick, and Julian.

"Well, where are they?" George said, looking up at the loft.

"Is anybody here?" Juan asked Samantha, staring at her glowing Vest.

Samantha's face went white, but she didn't get a chance to tell her friends what her Vest was telling her. Out of the shadows emerged three seven-foot, grotesque looking dinosaurs. They crept slowly forward, slapping their jaws together in a sort of frightening language.

"Well, if it isn't the three Vests . . . the new Brilliants," came Strength's voice from above.

He jumped down from the loft and landed a few feet away. A blur of black light skidded out of the shadows and then stopped next to Strength. Imagination was grinning viciously as he climbed out from behind an old stack of baled hay.

"The Chest picks them younger every time," Strength said, a thin-lipped grin forming.

Samantha, George, and Juan were so terrified they couldn't speak. To make things worse, the sun disappeared behind a group of thick clouds, and the bright light dwindled away. When their eyes had adjusted, they saw the bodies of the slain victims across the barn floor.

Samantha screamed and brought her hand up to her mouth. One of the dinosaurs took this movement as aggression and lunged for her but was rebuked by Imagination and stepped back, its wicked eyes fixed on Samantha.

Juan's knees were shaking, and his stomach felt as though someone was squeezing it like a sponge. George's lips were quivering so hard his teeth were chattering.

"Your Envoys who were supposed to meet you," Strength said lowly, pointing at the lifeless bodies. "They were sent to brief you, but I think I'll take over from here. Let's see, what would they say . . . hmmm . . . they would say you are Brilliants. You are part of an elite group dedicated to helping others. Isn't that sweet?" Strength looked at Imagination and Speed, who leered back at him.

"But you see there's another elite group, a more powerful group — and that's who stands before you now. We are the Shadows. We are the ones who destroy the Brilliants. We are . . ."

Samantha couldn't hear what Strength was saying. She felt like she was going to faint. The barn was spinning and her mouth watering, as though she was about to throw up. Then she heard her Vest, like a voice in a dream from faraway telling her the same thing — CONCENTRATE ON IMAGINATION. CONCENTRATE!

Samantha looked over at Imagination who stood fixed with an evil smile stamped on his fat face. She concentrated on him. What about him? His power — what made his power? And then it came to her, and she shouted in a frenzied voice, "Don't believe! Don't believe!"

Strength stopped talking.

"The dinosaurs aren't real unless you believe! Don't believe, and they won't be real! They'll go away!"

"Silence!" Imagination shouted, but it didn't help because Juan, George, and Samantha no longer believed the dreamed-up creatures were real, and they vanished in an explosion of dark light.

Samantha's shout was the bolt of courage George and Juan needed. They donned their Vests, and George lifted into the air, swung his foot as hard as he could, and caught the charging Imagination in the face, knocking him to the ground.

Juan disappeared and ran to his left. Speed reacted by moving at George, but George was too high and ascending higher. Strength's attention was directed toward George and therefore, didn't see the pitchfork jousting toward his leg. By the time he realized what was happening, one of the tines had gone completely through his kneecap.

He screamed and turned his leg so that he could reach the handle, and then broke it off like it was a toothpick. Blood oozed down his leg, and he gritted his teeth as he pulled the pitchfork completely out with one big jerk.

Imagination got to his feet, still a little dazed. George swooped down in an attempt to pick up Samantha, but Speed was too fast and pulled him to the ground by his shirt, wrestling him until finally pinning him down.

Strength stared savagely at Samantha. He took two steps toward her and wrapped his massive fingers around her neck.

"Go visible boy or I'll crush her neck," he said enraged.

Samantha was trembling. George was trying to

struggle free but it was no use.

"On the count of three, boy. One . . . two . . ."

To his left, Strength watched Juan materialize. Imagination ran to him and grabbed him by the arm.

"I don't care what Melt wants," Strength spat, "these three die with the others!"

What happened next occurred so fast that no one was ready for it.

A bright, white light lit up the barn so intensely that everyone had to close their eyes. When the light subsided, a thick, white smoke was misting two feet above the ground like it was alive. Standing almost directly in the middle of the old barn was a man wearing a robe that sparkled and crackled like fire. Bursts of light exploded everywhere on it. Even his mop of gray hair sparkled with light.

The man had a look of cold fury. His sky-blue eyes were narrowed; his lips were pursed. Samantha, George, and Juan sensed an incredible feeling of comfort surround them as he stepped forward. He raised his right hand and Strength was sent reeling backward, like he'd been hit by a small truck.

The robed man turned his attention to Speed who stood thunderstruck. Suddenly, a bubble of white light engulfed him like a small prison. He began shouting and pounding on it, but it was as though it was made of some unbreakable, soundproof material. No one could hear his screams.

Imagination made a run for the opening in the barn wall, but a white bubble encompassed him, too. Strength grunted and managed to get his feet, still dazed from the Robe's blast.

"Robe," he said, hobbling. "You . . . but you never help. . . ."

Another bubble of light appeared, this time trapping Strength. The Robe moved forward past Samantha and faced the bubble that held the strong man. It wasn't until then that Samantha noticed the stranger was floating a few inches above the ground.

"Derrick Mendas, you were given the Gift of Strength. Now I take it from you, and you will join the others in banishment."

When the Robe spoke, his words echoed loudly. Suddenly Samantha, with the help of her Vest, realized that this was the same voice that had come out of the Chest in Boulder Cave.

Strength looked terrified, his eyes bulging, his mouth open in a silent scream as his Vest of Dark Light dissolved and the bubble of light exploded. The Robe turned to Speed, who was holding his hands out in front of him, waving them frantically.

"Argus Nelly, you were given the Gift of Speed. Now I take it from you, and you will join the others in Banishment," the Robe said, and the bubble that housed Speed exploded.

The Robe then turned, ignoring George, Samantha, and Juan, and floated over to face Imagination's bubble. The fury in the Robe's eyes earlier was nothing compared to the look of fire he had as he stared at Imagination in utter loathing.

"Imagination . . . you, I do not banish . . . but you . . ."

The bubble of light dissolved away, and Imagination found himself standing face to face. The Robe held out his left hand, and Imagination wailed in pain, grabbing his hip.

". . . you will suffer — suffer your entire existence for the lives you took today."

Red, giant boils began to surface on Imagination's skin until he was covered with them like giant chicken pox. "And you will not speak again. You will be ridiculed and alone for the rest of your life. Kyle Gainly, you killed three innocent children today. Now I take your power, and condemn you to live your life in suffering."

Kyle Gainly barely looked human. He opened his mouth to speak, but there was nothing. He looked terrified, and he felt his skin. The boils were everywhere — on his arms, on his neck, all over his face. He turned and limped ever so slowly and laboriously toward the opening in the barn wall until finally he was out of sight.

The Robe turned and glided over to Luis first, looking at the boy's limp body. He raised his hand and a sparkling blanket of light wrapped around him, and then disappeared. When it had gone, Luis still lay silent, but the wounds and bloodstains inflicted by Imagination's dinosaurs were no longer visible.

The Robe moved over to Jannick, raised his right hand, and a blanket appeared over him as well, healing his wounds. The Robe moved to Julian and did the same until Julian's face and neck had been restored.

There was silence, the kind where there are no words to say because language can't be used to define the moment. The Robe stared at the three lifeless bodies, and Samantha could sense the immense pain he was feeling for them.

When the Robe turned and faced George, Samantha, and Juan, his eyes were much calmer and somber.

"You have questions," he spoke slowly. "Sit down. I will stay with you awhile and answer some of them."

George and Juan sat, but Samantha remained standing, examining the robe the man was wearing as it sparkled and crackled like fire. "Why do you have a robe, and we have

Vests?" she wondered.

"Good question, Samantha. I have more power and experience than you, therefore I have a robe."

Samantha wasn't sure if this answer confused her more, but she moved on. "Who were those men? And why'd they kill those boys?"

The Robe looked to the ground for a moment and sighed deeply. "Those men were once Brilliants, like yourselves, but they changed. They used their powers for the wrong things, and they turned to the Dark Vests. They killed these boys because the Shadows want all of the Brilliants destroyed. It never used to be like that. There was never death. There were never Dark Vests until Xylo changed all that. But I'm afraid if I continue, I'll just confuse you more."

George stood up before asking his question. He didn't know why, but it just felt like that was what he was supposed to do before addressing the man. "Those guys had been following us hadn't they? I saw Speed along the dike by my house one night."

"Yes, he was scouting your house. They were following you everywhere using Imagination's power. They were above you the night you went to the Point, concealed in an imaginary rock."

"How did you know we went there?"

The Robe smiled. "I know."

"Those things that attacked these boys and went after us were just fake? They came from Imagination's mind?" Juan, now standing, wasn't sure he completely understood.

"Imagination's power was mighty when a person didn't know its weakness. Most believe what they see. For the boys, the creatures he created out of his mind were real, but Samantha was right in figuring out that his power only worked if you believed what he created was real. When you don't believe, they no longer exist."

There was silence again. George, Samantha, and Juan had other questions, but none were coming to mind. The Robe began to ascend into the air, looking at them with compassion. "What you need now is time. You've seen too much, too soon. It was never meant to be that way. Whenever there are new Brilliants, like yourselves, we like to give you time to learn about your powers and Gifts on your own, and I suspect the Maker will do the same with you."

"What do you mean?" Samantha pleaded, stepping forward and raising her arm toward the Robe. "Who's the Maker?"

But the Robe only smiled wider. "Your questions will be answered in time. You must learn more about the Gifts that have been given to you. But be warned — do not let your Vests become dark like the ones you saw here today. Listen to your Vests, for they will guide you in times of trouble; ignore them, and you will suffer the same fate as the men you saw here today."

"Where did those men go? What's banishment?" Samantha was desperate.

"All in time, young Samantha Banks. You must have patience, but I will give you something that will help you, to be with you in your greatest times of need."

The Robe raised his left arm, and an arrow of light formed in midair in front of his fingers. It shot down and penetrated Samantha's Vest of Light, lodging itself in her shoulder. Samantha felt no pain as she watched the Vest suck it in like a whirlpool.

"What was that?" she called, but the Robe's smile had gone. He was now lifting his other arm, and as he did, the bodies of Luis, Jannick, and Julian were raised, hovering above the ground and covered in a bubble of light.

"I have to go and inform parents that their sons were killed for no reason, that they were killed because they were good. It was never meant to be this way," the Robe said, almost talking to himself now.

In a flash of white light, he and the three boys vanished. The barn was silent. Everyone stood staring up at the loft where the Robe had been, all of them with questions that would not be answered.

"That could've been us," George said seriously.

"Almost was," whispered Samantha, still staring at the loft.

"Who was he?"

"I don't know. My Vest isn't telling me anything about him, or about any of the questions I have about all of this. But I can tell you, the Robe is powerful."

"Oh, yeah," George affirmed. "Did you see the way he created those bubbles and trapped those guys?"

"Big time," Juan agreed. "And did you see Imagination? I wouldn't want to be that guy."

"I had all of these questions I wanted to ask, but I kept going blank," George said, angry with himself. "Like the Chest we saw in Boulder Cave — where did it come from? And what was the Robe's power? It seemed like he had more than just one Gift."

"Yes, for sure —" Samantha nodded.

"So what do we do?" George asked, squeezing his hands together.

"We give it time," Samantha answered. "We just have to give it time."

For the next several minutes they said nothing.

"C'mon. Let's go," Samantha finally suggested, walking over to the large pink elephant she had won at the ring toss.

Grinning, she dusted it off and stroked its head.

* * *

Kristina Gonzalez was sound asleep when she heard the faint tapping that seemed to be part of the dream she was having about playing basketball with Mike Johnson, her wishful boyfriend. But the knocking grew louder and she could hear her name being called. The voice got loud enough to awaken her, but she lie silent, her eyes moving back and forth in the dark, listening — then the knocking came again. She drew in a nervous breath and raised her head. Someone was knocking on her second-story bedroom window. She propped herself up with her elbows and reached over to her nightstand, flipping on the light.

She looked toward the window and squinted. What she was seeing couldn't be. This was no dream, but how . . .

Kristina moved closer, and as she did, it became clearer. Sitting on the roof outside her bedroom window was a giant pink elephant, just like the one she tried to win every year at the fair. She opened the window and looked around. How could it have gotten there? There was no one around, yet there sat the stuffed animal she had yearned for every year. She grabbed it, pulled it inside and began to laugh, looking at it as if it was the most precious gift she had ever received.

High above, and concealed behind the massive tall branches of an overhanging pine, Samantha smiled. She was straddling George's back and holding on to Juan who was sitting in front of her.

"Look at her," George said with a grin.

"I wonder what she's thinking," Juan said, chuckling.

"She's wondering how that ended up in front of her window at midnight." Samantha couldn't help giggling. "And she loves it."

Kristina's bedroom light clicked off, her room once again dark. George moved out from behind the tree limbs and soared above her house, staring down at the rows of homes that lined the street. The evening was warm, unusually warm for the end of September, and George flew slowly, circling around and heading toward Samantha's home.

"Let's just fly a little tonight," Samantha said, gazing down below at the hundreds of lights that flooded the night sky.

"Yeah, let's just fly," Juan agreed, feeling the gentle

breeze push against his face.

George nodded and continued to sail silently through the night, his two friends on his back.

"We're a part of something now," Juan said quietly after a few minutes. "We're part of something that's really good."

"And really bad," Samantha added soberly.

But just how bad and just how good, none of them knew.

Only time would tell.

THE END

Learn more about the 3V World at:
www.threevests.com

About the Author

Robert Bowman has taught elementary, middle, and high school for over eight years in north central Washington state. He enjoys steelhead fishing and writing in his spare time.

The Three Vests started as a classroom story in 1997. This is Mr. Bowman's first children's novel.

About the Cover Artist

Craig Mullins is an acclaimed digital matte painter, conceptual artist, and illustrator, receiving his graduate degree in illustration in 1989. His work has been featured in a wide variety of entertainment projects including feature films, commercials and specialty films.

In his infrequent spare time, Craig enjoys windsurfing and gardening. You can learn more about Craig and his work at: www.goodbrush.com.

Ordering Information:

Smart and Smarter Publishing
Toll Free: 1-877-807-3703

www.smartandsmarter.com

"Sir? Are you sure?"

"Yes, Melt. Finally, we have a Musicular."